AMAZING GRACE

Holloway House Originals
by Odie Hawkins

CHESTER L. SIMMONS
CHICAGO HUSTLE
GHETTO SKETCHES
MENFRIENDS
PORTRAIT OF SIMONE
SCARS AND MEMORIES
SECRET MUSIC
SWEET PETER DEEDER
THE BUSTING OUT OF AN ORDINARY MAN
THE MEMOIRS OF A BLACK CASANOVA
THE LIFE AND TIMES OF CHESTER L. SIMMONS
BLACK CHICAGO
BRAZILIAN NIGHTS
CONSPIRACY
AMAZING GRACE

AMAZING GRACE

ODIE HAWKINS

Originally published by Holloway House Publishing Co.

Front cover photo by Zola Salena-Hawkins,
www.flickr.com/photos/32886903@N02

Copyright © 1993, 2012 by Odie Hawkins

ISBN: 978-1-5040-3579-8

Distributed in 2016 by Open Road Distribution
180 Maiden Lane
New York, NY 10038
www.openroadmedia.com

To Nana Okyere Bekoe II,
with love

AMAZING GRACE

Queen of the Projects

"Shhhhh!"

"What? What is it?"

"I thought I heard something."

Someone trying to break in? Diana having another bad dream? Charles stumbling to the toilet half asleep?

"What is it, baby?"

"Edward, please don't call me 'baby,' it sounds so vulgar."

The normal noises of the Cabrini-Taylor projects continued to accompany their weekly sexual get together: doors slamming, boom boxes blaring raps, screams, yells, car horns blasting, sirens screeling, police helicopters clattering overhead, crashing sounds, summertime noises in the projects—Mondays, Tuesdays, Wednesdays, Thursdays, Fridays, Saturdays, Sundays.

"Are you finished?"

Elizabeth Mayflower fixed the face above her in her near-sighted vision. Must get some glasses soon.

"How 'bout you, baby, did you...?"

"You'd really like to know that, wouldn't you?"

She shook the large-boned man straddling her off of her body like a shaggy dog shaking water from its coat and reached over to take a terry cloth towel from a bedside table.

She reached down underneath the thin summer cover and swabbed the sexual juice between her legs, a disgusted expression on her face, and suddenly, with a chameleon-like smile, grabbed her partner's penis and ground the head with the rough cloth as though it were a skillet with stubborn stains.

"Hey! Be careful! That thing is real tender."

She carefully placed the towel underneath her hips to catch any drainoff and laid back with her hands folded across her stomach.

"You wanna cuddle up in my arms?"

"No."

They lay side by side, each preoccupied with their own thoughts.

"Liz?"

"Elizabeth, Edward, Elizabeth. How many times must I tell you not to call me Liz?! Sounds like something you'd call a cow!"

The man was reduced to silence again. She had all the answers and with that English accent she sounded so right, even when she was dead wrong.

The flashing lights of a passing ambulance flickered across the ceiling, the piercing siren penetrated the room. She could feel the man becoming aroused again.

"Elizabeth...?"

"Edward, it's getting rather late..."

He leaned up on his elbow and gave her a mean look.

10

"You wanna kiss me goodbye?"

"Yes, yes I do."

His mean look surrendered to a surprised expression as her arms circled his shoulders and pulled him to her bosom.

Her kissing was warm and deep, loving.

Elizabeth Mayflower is just full of tricks 'n turns; just when I got her figured to do one thing she'll up 'n do the exact opposite. Guess it must be that English in her.

She gently pushed him away from her as he attempted to mount her again.

"No, Edward, please don't..."

He didn't insist and slowly sat up on the side of the bed.

She stared affectionately at his broad back...

What a good man he is, so warm and so considerate.

She watched his silhouette in the dark room as he pulled on his shorts, pants, socks and shoes, buttoned his shirt.

"Liz...Elizabeth? You sleep?" he whispered in her ear.

"No, but I will be shortly."

"I'm leaving. What I wanted to ask was whether or not you'd like to go to the park on Saturday, with the kids. Maybe we could barbecue some ribs. You know, have a picnic?"

"Call me later in the week."

"I will. 'Night. I love you, Elizabeth."

He planted a wet, clumsy kiss on her mouth and felt his way to the bedroom door.

"Don't forget to put the locked position on the knob."

"I won't. Talk to you tomorrow."

She lay in bed for a few minutes after her lover's exit and got up to check the lock.

One can't be too careful in the projects. After checking the door (he had locked it), she tiptoed to her children's room.

Diana, in the bottom half of the bunk bed, was curled into her usual ladylike knot. Charles was sprawled across the top bunk.

11

Such beautiful children, I must say, even if they are mine.

She left her children's room and went into the toilet to urinate and brush her teeth.

She stared at her body in the mirror above the washbasin. Nice breasts, a bit pendulous, but nice.

Stomach fairly smooth, no stretch marks after two children. Do abortions create stretch marks? Ten pounds too much, but shapely. She turned to study her profile.

A true kaffir arse, they would say.

She gave herself an affectionate pat on both buttocks.

Well, even with the British accent, they could never accuse me of trying to pass for white.

She sprawled on her bed, remembering to keep the towel under her.

Edward has so much sperm. The man is like a fountain of cum. She closed her eyes and felt the place he had been in.

He's so big I feel like he's stretching me. She dabbed her ring finger into her moist slit. Now she could surrender to her feelings.

There was no one there to record her reactions, no one to take advantage of her feelings. She heard herself moaning and clamped her left hand over her mouth as she continued milking her vagina, tickling her clitoris.

The release was soft, intense, and left her feeling satisfied, complete. She drew the towel up between her legs and cradled her head in her hands.

A flurry of pistol shots tensed her neck. Someone firing an Uzi. A drug deal gone sour? After two years in the Cabrini-Taylor Homes she could distinguish the difference between the rapid popping of the Uzi automatic machine gun and a number of other automatic weapons.

Shotguns were becoming popular and several people had recently been destroyed by Desert Storm hand grenades.

Tears suddenly mingled with the lascivious emissions.

12

God, why does this man tell me that he loves me? How can he love me? I don't even come off with him. Or give him a decent lay. How can he say, "I love you?"

A picnic on Saturday? No doubt he'll have his mum make a mountain of that bloody potato salad with jars of mayo in it. And then we'll go out to burn up half a cow, slather it with that horrible bar-be-cue sauce that he loves, and swat mosquitoes until it's time to return to the noise.

She winced at the sounds of people arguing loudly someplace near her window.

Love? "I love you, Elizabeth."

What does Edward know about love? I have two children and an abortion in between to prove that I know what love is. What do they know, other than pushing it in and pulling it out? What do they know about romantic feelings?

London in the spring, strolling through Windsor Park, watching the changing of the Guard, seeing the Queen on the Palace balcony.

Images, reflections. She closed her eyes and smiled, recalling how pleasant life had been in London, England.

Yes, there was color prejudice there and I am Black, an African almost, with a half-Nigerian father and a half-Ghanaian mother, God rest their souls. But it wasn't this bloody stuff.

The popping of a revolver and the screeching of car wheels turning a corner barely caused her to pay any attention. What the bloody hell, let them do whatever. . .

Why not go back to England?

She turned the notion around in her head once again, rejecting it, once again.

Diana and Charles would never have the opportunities back there that they have here, beyond Cabrini-Taylor.

She nodded off, alert to the unusual sounds, noises. Must remember to put another lock on the front door.

13

The difference between morning sounds in the Cabrini-Taylor Homes and night sounds was slight. There were fewer gunfights, usually, but more music from the hundreds of ghetto blasters, each of them seemingly tuned to a different station.

Bright sunlight filtered through her heavily starched kitchen curtains. Another day in the projects.

"Diana, don't put your face down in your cereal bowl like that, it doesn't look nice."

"Yes, Mommy."

"Charles, did you iron your shirt? It looks a bit wrinkled about the shoulders."

"I ironed it, Mom."

"Well, next time iron it better. It doesn't look very nice."

"Yes, Mom."

Elizabeth Mayflower leaned back in her breakfast nook, proudly surveying her children and her surroundings. The children were polite and well behaved; the two bedroom, second story apartment immaculate.

If only I can hang on to this part-time job long enough and finish out the food service course at Bradley Junior College, we can move to a proper apartment.

"Mommy? Mommy?"

"Yes, Diana, what is it?"

"What time did Mr. Winsor leave last night?"

Were they exchanging smirks?

"Uhh, shortly after you two went to bed. Now then, if you're finished with your cereal, rinse your bowls out and get ready for the camp bus. It'll be here in fifteen minutes."

Her children dutifully rinsed their cereal bowls out and packed their backpacks with a lunch of bran biscuits ("don't you dare eat any of those dreadful white bread sandwiches they pass out. You may have fruit.") filled with marmalade and an apple each.

She held a final inspection of shoes, socks, shorts and shirts just before they left.

They embraced her spontaneously, warmly, before leaving to catch the day camp bus ("Mount Holyoke Day Camp, we care.") for a day of play in the park, a trip to the Museum of Science and Industry, a visit to a historical landmark, or maybe a day in the woods.

She leaned out of her window to watch them walk to the corner pickup point.

"Charles, hold Diana's hand!"

The usual assembly of winos, drug addicts, drifters, gangbangers and unemployed nodded pleasantly at the children. One of the men called up to Elizabeth.

"Hi you doin' today, Miss Queen?!"

"Quite well, thank you," she answered in an even voice.

She drew her head back inside the window and watched her children through a slit in the curtain. The bus was on time.

She settled back with a second cup of tea, relieved that her children were free of the projects for another day.

Life in the projects was a different version of hell. There were times when she felt affection for the people around her, who were willing to help her at any time.

"Now, we know you new here, 'Lizabeth, so don't hesitate if you need something, okay?"

And there were other times when she hated them. She hated the petty rivalries, the schizoid attitudes, the casual way of life that gave everybody a nickname: "Big Nuts" was one of the gangleaders, "Slobber Lips Sally," the twenty year old wino who looked to be fifty, "Crackhead," "Blue," "Icebag Charley," the heroin pusher who had sold killer bags of heroin to three junkies in the past year, Edward/Eddie "Killer Boy" Winsor, the man in her life.

They had dubbed her "Queen" because of her fastidious

15

habits and attitude.

Tuesday, an "off" day. So much to do and yet none of it seemed to take her anywhere. Ironing today, washing tomorrow after work, house cleaning, buying food miles away because the stores in the immediate neighborhood only stocked sugar-based foods.

"God, what is it about sugar that turns poor people on so?"

Night classes at Bradley, starting in September. Stupid. What the hell is so complicated about serving bean soup that you'd have to go to college for?

The rationale behind the program was to encourage "project people" to go to school. She understood that, but why twenty-six weeks?

Monday and Friday, working four hours each day at the Featherstone Institute was ten times more "educational" than classes at Bradley Junior College would ever be.

There was no doubt in her mind that they had hired her as a "custodial consultant" because of her British accent.

"And you're from England?"

"Yes, mum. London to be exact."

She had played the interview "to the busstop," as some of her project girlfriends put it.

"Play it to the busstop! Whatever gits you over gits you over!"

Featherstone Institute gave her eight hours each week to check out how the "other half" lived. Or suffered.

The Institute was a treatment center for rich women who were bulimic. Or anorexic. Or simply bored.

Oh well, time to stop wool gathering. She pulled the ironing board from the hall closet and a basket of clothes to be ironed from the children's room.

Ironing was an exercise in self-control for her because she hated ironing.

The soft triple knocking on the door meant that Mary

16

Margaret was paying her a visit. She continued struggling to iron the pleats in Diana's skirt for a few moments. The triple knocking tripled persistently.

"Yes, who is it?" she asked, checking the fisheye peephole at the same time.

"Me, Mary Margaret," came the slurred answer.

Elizabeth opened the door, ushered her visitor to a seat at the dinette table, closed the door ceremoniously and continued ironing, defying Mary Margaret to interrupt her routine.

"Yooooohh, girlfriend! Looks like you're tryin' to flatten a few things out, huh?"

Elizabeth looked up from her ironing and smiled affectionately at Mary Margaret (everyone was reminded by Mary Margaret to call her "Mary Margaret").

"I suppose one could say that."

"Well, I don't know what *one* could say, but that's what I'm sayin'..."

Mary Margaret's overextended, high pitched laughter indicated that she was semi-drunk. She never seemed to be totally sober.

"Yeahhh...I saw you wavin' yo' kids off to day camp so I figured you was off today."

Elizabeth acknowledged the information with a stiff nod and became more methodical in her ironing.

"Yes, Mary Margaret, it's Tuesday and I'm off. What're you up to?"

"Well, not a helluva lot," was the immediate response.

She composed a neutral expression as she watched Mary Margaret draw a bottle of cheap gin from her purse.

What the bloody hell could be happening in your bloody mind to find it necessary to get blotto before noon?

"Mary Margaret, would you care for a spot of tea?"

"Oh, thank you, deah gurl, that would be scrumptious,"

17

she answered in a broad, fake accent. Her neighbors enjoyed putting her on and, since the teasing wasn't malicious, she took it graciously.

She reheated the teapot, focusing on how much ironing she had to do. Mary Margaret was an obstacle, not a dividend.

She poured her guest a cup of tea and returned to her ironing board. Mary Margaret took a lip-searing sip, poured some of the offending liquid into the kitchen sink and added two fingers of cheap gin to the brew.

"Hope you don't mind, girlfriend, it's kinda hot." Mary Margaret fancied herself being the journalist who was going to write "The Elizabeth Mayflower Story."

Hey, sister, look at it f' real. How many Black women can you think of who've had the kind of experiences in life that you've had? I mean, hey, shit, they got people who would pay to read about yo' shit."

"But Mary Margaret, let's face it, we have people who have much more exciting things happen in their lives every day."

"Yeahhh, but they ain't in the fuckin' projects."

Sometimes Mary Margaret came with a three-ringed notebook, ballpoint pen and a half pint of gin.

Most often she only came with a half pint of gin. No one had ever seen any evidence of her writing.

"I don't wanna show off."

Elizabeth ironed her children's clothes, ignoring Mary Margaret's presence. She knew how to deal with the visiting party lover.

"'Lizabeth, I want you to explain to me one thang—how in the hell did you wind up in Cabrini-Taylor, number one, and number two, I saw what's-his-name sneaking outta here last night...heeheehee."

Mary Margaret knew what it took to ring Elizabeth

18

Mayflower's bell. She stood the iron up on end and pursed her lips for a moment before speaking.

"I'm certain I must've told you at least a thousand times how I came to live here in Cabrini.

"Now, then, insofar as Edward is concerned, that's nobody's concern but my own."

She thought it was simply amazing, the way people came on to her. People she felt no special sense of friendship with asked her the most intimate questions.

"How old are you, E-liza-bit?"

"Her friend," Mary Margaret, took it a step beyond.

"The way I'd write it is the story of a fucked-up Black woman from England, with two illegitimate children, okay?—who comes to the United States and gets stiffed off by her would-be jive ass relatives and winds up in urban purgatory." That was the fascinating thing about Mary Margaret: If you hung on, she'd give you a word that pulled your head around.

Purgatory? Urban purgatory?

"We'd have to get a few things straightened out before you started writing the Mayflower story. First, I should like you to understand that I am not a 'fucked-up' Black woman from England, and secondly, children, no matter how they get here, are not illegitimate."

Once again, Mary Margaret fixed a sly smile on her face.

"Uuhh, ooohh, pressed your button, didn't I?"

Elizabeth returned the smile. Yes, you did press my button, you ignorant drunk bitch.

"'Lizabeth? Don't you watch TV when you iron? That's what I do when I'm ironin'. It distracts me."

Mary Margaret was filled with twists, turns, sudden countermotions.

"I watch television very seldom, usually for a few hours."

She moved the iron back and forth methodically, paused

19

to glare defiantly into her neighbor's face.

"Ain't no need to get yo' tailfeathers ruffled, I was just askin', that's all."

Elizabeth hung Diana's ruffled dress on a hanger and pulled Charles' blue shirt out of the laundry basket, feeling slightly pissed. Why couldn't the bloody woman simply sit and drink her bloody gin without interfering in her bloody business?

"Mary, how are things going with you and Jack?"

She felt the best thing to do was shift to something neutral. Mary Margaret made a wry face.

"Awwww, you know how it is with us, same ol' same ol'. I don't wanna talk about him. Let's git back to the TV thing. You say you *never* watch TV during the week?!"

"Very seldom, maybe a special of some sort."

Mary Margaret tipped another hook of gin into her teacup.

"That means you missin' a whole lotta Oprah, G-raldo, Dona-hoo, people like that."

"And just what am I missing? A bunch of miserable people talking about their bloody miserable lives? Don't we have enough misery around us already? Why should I watch it on television?"

"You mean to say you don't let your kids watch cartoons?"

There were days when a visit from Mary Margaret could be an entertaining diversion; this wasn't one of those days. Elizabeth felt a bit edgier than usual.

Dammit! I hope I'm not pregs, that's all I'd need right now. I don't think I could stand another abortion.

"No, Mary Margaret, I don't allow my children to watch cartoons, they're too many commercials suggesting things to them that I feel are unhealthy and stupid."

"Like what?"

Mary Margaret was literally in her cups, enjoying the exchange without caring where it was going. A sudden louder

20

than usual noise pulled both of them to look out of the window.

The crowd below, milling around in the community quadrangle, cocooned two muscular young fighting men. One of them had a long butcher knife, the other one swung a length of link chain. The butcher knife flashed from side to side, catching the glare of the sun.

The man with the chain whirled it desperately, his face contorted by his fear.

Elizabeth and Mary Margaret folded their arms and settled their elbows on the window sill. It was a gruesome sight to watch, and irresistible.

Elizabeth felt like screaming, "Stop! Stop fighting! For God's sake! Please stop fighting!" but she knew it would be useless. The crowd had boxed the men in and they would only be satisfied by the sight of blood.

Tears riveleted Mary Margaret's face as she spoke. "God! I hate to see these young brothers out here killin' each other like this."

Elizabeth draped her arm around her girlfriend's shoulder. Mary Margaret wasn't the tough cookie she seemed to be.

They both flinched at the sight of the chain cracking across the knife man's face and the sudden flush of blood that oozed from his eye and cheek.

A neighbor in the next window called out in a casual voice, "Anybody call the po-lease?"

None of the others leaning out of their windows answered. Elizabeth dashed away from her window to dial 911. Who knows! Maybe they'll come this time.

Cabrini-Taylor had such a bad reputation that the police were reluctant to come into the middle of these slabs of concrete. They circled the perimeters and maintained a buffer zone between Cabrini-Taylor and the upper middle class condo development to the east of the projects.

"Yes, two men are fighting with weapons, please hurry!"

She slammed the phone down—hope they don't think someone is playing a joke—and rushed back to the window.

Mary Margaret pointed unnecessarily at the man with the chain sprawled out on the pavement.

He was bleeding from stab wounds to his throat, chest and stomach. A trail of blood showed the direction the man with the butcher knife had fled.

A tight knot of concerned people were trying to stop the flow of blood from the man on the pavement, with handkerchiefs, bath towels.

The police arrived within minutes, miraculously. And a few minutes later, the ambulance, popularly called "the meat wagon."

The crowd reappeared, edging in to take a last look at the wounded man. The police asked a few random questions, made a few notes, but it was obvious that they didn't feel that anything extraordinary had happened.

Elizabeth returned to her ironing board, unnerved by the brutal sight of the bleeding figure carried away in "the meat wagon."

She didn't feel like ironing, she felt like going to her bedroom and curling into a knot to cry. She felt as though she wanted to blot everything out.

Mary Margaret left the window, poured the dregs of the half pint bottle into her cup and slumped into a chair.

"Makes you mad, you know what I mean? To be seein' these young brothers kill each other up like that."

Elizabeth continued pressing clothes for a few more minutes. It was important to maintain discipline. She knew she would break down if she stopped ironing.

It was important to finish simple tasks in the projects, to keep "a stiff upper lip," as it were.

Mary Margaret once spoke about how much she disliked

22

the taste of gin at one point in her life.

"Nothin' in the world tasted worse to me, nothin'!"

Mary Margaret's discipline slipped and she continued tasting and sipping until the gin became tasty to her.

Another one of the girlfriends, Lila Perry, a third generation project dweller, described her grandmother talking about getting out of the projects.

"She could never make herself believe that she was really livin' in the projects, number one. You know what I mean? A young woman from a small town in Miss'sippi? I think my mom felt pretty much the same way."

Tanisha Sanders, at twenty-four, the youngest of Elizabeth's "inner circle," was another "disbeliever."

"I'm much too slick for this shit! You think I'm gon' raise my children in the midst of all this madness, you're outta your mind!"

She finished ironing a pair of Charles' blue jeans, her hands shaking.

Mary Margaret's shrewd expression melted into a compassionate one.

"Nawww, girlfriend, we don't need no mo' gin. You don't need mo' at all and I definitely don't need no mo'."

She stood unsteadily and shuffled to the door with as much dignity as she could manage.

"Well, girlfriend, guess we've had as much excitement as we can handle for one day, huh? I best be gittin' on, got stuff to do, you know? I might try to write something about what we just saw."

Elizabeth blindsided her with a hug and a peck on the cheek at the door. They held each other at arm's length for a moment, unable to find words for what they felt.

The apartment was much emptier after Mary Margaret's exit, but not quieter. The horrible scene that had happened a few minutes earlier seemed to stir up the music, boost the

23

decibel levels of the noise elements around her.

Were people feeling more aroused because they had witnessed the shedding of blood?

She disconnected the iron and felt suddenly disconnected herself. She stood, leaning on the ironing board with a vacant look in her eyes.

Vivid thoughts flashed behind the vacant look: Should I lose my British accent?

"Why, what can I say? The bitch is just different, you know what I mean? She makes you feel like you doin' somethin' wrong, like you're dissin' her if you don't take off your hat when you git up in her place.

"She took 'Killer Boy' Winsor and turned him into a punk. Now, hey, don't be goin' around tellin' everybody what I said, okay?"

"I became her first friend when she moved up in here. I could tell she was freaked out by the scene. So I went up to her place and knocked real gentle-like.

" 'Hello,' I said when she came to the door. 'My name is Mary Margaret Smith. I'm your neighbor.' I knew there was something different about her the second she opened her mouth.

"I thought she was playin' some kind of joke on me, talkin' like that. Or maybe that gin had done a number on the back of my brain.

"We got to knowin' each other pretty good, after awhile.

"Like, I mean, I'd drop in on her every other day, you know, just to check her out.

"Stubborn sister, I gotta tell you, fulla strange ideas about what you should eat 'n shit.

"I mean, like, hey, check it out...she won't even allow her children to watch TV. But she's nice. She'll share her

24

last dime with you."

She stumbled away from the ironing board feeling drunk. Why am I considered some sort of freak because my place is neat and clean and I insist on maintaining control of my children?

She brewed herself a cup of tea and sat staring out of the window at the puddles of blood on the pavement beneath her. The blood had a glazed look, almost a design on the ground.

Well, this is one we were privileged to watch. Most of the time we have to hide from the bullets.

She sipped her tea, ironing placed on hold for the moment.

Mary Margaret writing a book? Am I practicing for my debut at the Met?

Lila and Tanisha. Do they really think they're going to be able to pull themselves out of this swamp? Will I make it?

That was one of the things they all hated most about the projects: the uncertainty of life. And the boredom.

Despite the fights, the drugs, the shootings, life was boring in the projects. She couldn't put the contradiction to rest.

Murders are happening every day but the place is a crashing bore. Maybe the boredom comes from the monotony of the violence, so much of the same thing . . .

A woman with two small children walked past the bloody puddles, pausing to stare at the designs for a few moments.

The blood would probably be there until the next rain.

Edward? How can I love him when I have so little control of my life? So little love to offer.

The tears rolling over her cheeks surprised her. She immediately placed her half empty cup in the sink, marched to the ironing board and reconnected the iron.

Enough of this, I must remember who I am.

25

Lady Day

Some of the greatest dancers in the world live in the projects. They also sing. Some of them are young, some not so young, all of them share the horrors of life in the projects.

"Billie Holiday" lives on the tenth floor of one of the sandwiched boxes called the Robert Taylor Homes. "Billie" is twelve years old (looks about fourteen) and has been singing all her life. She sings from the time she wakes up 'til she goes to bed.

She sings commercials, popular songs, raps, whatever catches her head, but her personal preference is for the music of the late Lady Day, Billie Holiday.

"I don't know what it was about Billie Holiday that grabbed me."

"Billie" sits at the corner of an ancient dinette table (see the television program *Good Times* for a facsimile), her pregnant belly wedged between her and the table. From time to time she stares pensively down into the common quadrangle shared by all of the inmates.

Snatches of "Gloomy Sunday," "Don't Explain" and "Strange Fruit" spill out of her as naturally as the story of her life.

"My grandma lived in the projects. It's kinda hard to believe that any old person could live in the projects, you know?"

"Billie" is lovely, no doubt in anybody's mind about that, a charcoal colored Mende woman transported direct. The young man (twenty-six years old) who got her in a family way doesn't think she is quite as beautiful as she once was.

"Hey, don't get me wrong, I still think the girl is something special, but now, since she messed up and got pregnant 'n shit, she seems different. You know what I mean? She ain't as much fun as she used to be."

"No, I don't 'member my father too good. He's like a shadow in my life."

The grizzled old-timers pop into the "Holiday" apartment on the weekends (which are apt to start on Thursday), wine, beer, gin and whisky bottles held at port arms, loaded, thirsty for the sound of "Billie's" rendition of Billie's music.

"It's mostly the older people who want to hear me sing Billie Holiday's music. The younger people, my friends, they ain't into it, they say it's too slow 'n draggy."

She sits at the dinette table, her hands folded like a shy school girl, and sings, "Them that's got shall get, them that's not shall lose, so the Bible says, and it still is news.

"Mama may have, Papa may have, but God bless the child that's got his own..."

Some of the old Billie lovers have to dry their eyes, or take another suck on the wine before they feel capable of saying anything.

"That's her, baby, that's really her. You got Billie in your

27

soul.''

Sometimes they leave a few bills in the dish on the table. Some offer her a drink.

"No, thank you. It ain't good for the baby.''

"Yeah, it is something, ain't it? Ain't nobody on either side of our family can carry a tune in a bucket, and how she comes along.''

Robert Taylor Acrobats, an esoteric breed for whom the term "daring" is the least descriptive of their activities, swing from one tall building to the other, unconcerned about falling.

They don't hear "Billie" or care about Billie. Their only concern is with the width of the line and whether or not it will carry them to the transfer point of wires; the wire of powdered coke to the crystal form called "crack."

The chemists on the eighth floor, protected by a belligerent army of drug-sapped lookouts, mix and sample the latest dream stuff, euphemistically entitled, "happy shit.''

Boys and girls, some of them acting as lookouts for the makers of "happy shit," others into more legitimate forms of acting, form an effervescent base in the projects.

They are everywhere, posturing, preening, rehearsing, reciting their lines, trying out new versions of old stories on each other.

"Yo' momma so fat she cain't even walk.''

"Yeah, well you' momma so ugly she can't even catch a cold.''

Some days, in the muggy heat of a Chicago summertime, they seem like candy-stoked dervishes, whirling from one small theatre-in-the-round to the next theatre-in-the-round.

The whole project is a stage and they are the actors on it. Fifteen-year-olds pretend to be thirty, in order to join the gang and receive the protection that being in a gang grants the bad actor.

28

Robin Hoods do *not* take from the rich (in the projects) and give to the poor. They take from the poor and keep it.

Writers are a dime a dozen on these grounds, they write with their lips, they are lipwriters, story finders, as in "finders keepers, losers weepers."

They blend into the mix of poets, rappers, space agents, hypnotists, painters and lawyers, all elements of this volatile situation called the projects.

The projects were designed to oppress Black people in Chicago. Some dishonest believers lie and say: "The projects were created to give the low income people an opportunity to have a decent place to live."

The outrageous lie that acted as the catalyst for the development of the projects still earns a few innocents, but it doesn't wash well with the hip and the really intelligent.

The projects are civilian penitentiaries, the inmates are primarily women with children (a clever ordinance mandated the absence of men, fathers), the warden (the city) and a set of elaborately designed social circumstances keep a tight rein on the beast that rages within.

The projects are ugly and incur the animosity of any sensitive person who is forced to live there. The sensitive person, enraged by the architectural nightmare that stacks him/her layer upon layer, surrounded by meshed wire and designs that mock his/her sense of African aesthetics will, at the first opportunity, attempt to beautify, crucify, mutilate, draw or graffitize on the brutal walls around them.

All of the laboratory experiments that "ethics" prevent the morally conscious from carrying out in the sterile labs of the country are routinely conducted in the projects.

Project: What is the simple effect of caging ten thousand human beings layer upon layer? Within structures that create hate for one's surroundings.

Project: How long does it take to create antisocial behavior within artificially divided groups (gangs)?

Project: If men, fathers, are denied the traditional role of men, fathers, how will that affect the children?

Project: Are African-Americans capable of overcoming generations of life in the projects?

Project: If African-Americans are walled off, given the worst food possible, inferior educations, exceptionally negative images of themselves and excessive amounts of sugar, what will happen?

Drug experimentation is relentless, sustained and premeditated. We can be certain that most of the latest chemically based drugs are given their first tryout in the projects.

Project: What effect will the newest drug "1-2-3," one of those newly developed mind warpers, have on those in the twelve- to fifteen-year-old group?

Project: What happens to the moralities of Africans who resisted the immoralities inherent to slavery in America if they are walled into projects?

Project: How is it possible to imprint so completely that the youth of the projects will regard the Chicago Housing Authority as The Parent?

Project: How long will African-Americans submit to being projected?

We can be certain that most of the aforementioned project experiments have been conducted/are being conducted, and that others are certainly on the drawing board.

In some ways it seems entirely reasonable that the projects were specifically designed for the powers that be to run games on.

There was obviously one flaw in the design. They neglected to consider the art of the greatest dancers in Chicago, in the world. They didn't do enough research on the African women that they intended for the Kraal.

30

If the city planners for dysfunction of the project poor had paid any attention to the apartheid experience of Soweto, Cross Roads and a number of other Afrikaner experiments at social engineering, they would have realized that they were doomed to fail.

The women of the projects, like their sisters in similar circumstances in South Africa, are rocks that cannot be moved. They slip and slide on winter ice, wading through packed walls of tainted snow to bring their children bread. They scrape threadbare pots with magic spoons and produce hot soups.

In the summer, defying bullet-blizzards, they provide bulletproof vests for their children, made of Momma skin, the softest and most difficult to penetrate.

The most elaborately developed dances are reserved for the bureaucracy. Who can say when that particular time step was first performed to dazzle the social worker? Or why that ice cold shimmy was used to skirt the issue of man-loneliness on the application that boldly asks, "Are you now, or have you ever been...?"

Most of the dances are tightly structured, with an emphasis on economy of motion. No one can afford to use more energy than necessary. And the names are definitely indicative of what they are meant to express.

The latest dance is called "the Project Freedom Step." Some people say it resembles the Electric Slide...

The Cotton Field

Paul Vernon made a casual wave to his next door neighbor. Daniel O'Reilly wasn't the kind of neighbor he felt warm about. The bastard had glared at him from behind his blinds for six months after they moved into Beverly Shores.

O'Reilly returned his wave with a grimace that bordered on a smile. It was obvious that they didn't love each other.

Melvin Williams, his neighbor on the opposite side, a large-boned Black man who always seemed to be mowing his lawn, looked up from his lawnmower and offered Paul a warm welcome home.

"Just pullin' in, huh?"

"Yeah, got caught in traffic all the way."

"I know how that is."

"Cuttin' it down a little bit?"

"Yeahhh, you know how it is. If I don't keep it down, Lucille starts screamin' bloody murder."

"I heard that. Talk to you later."

He pulled his dark green BMW around into the alley, opened the electronically operated doors and stepped out of the car into a spotless garage.

Great to be home. Friday: No more office bullshit 'til Monday. Shower. A glass of chilled white wine. A little interplay with the kids. A serious conversation with Yvonne.

He strolled out of the garage, his suit jacket folded over his left forearm, alligator hide briefcase in his right hand.

"Paul, if you're going to be an executive, you must have an executive's briefcase."

He paused in the ten-yard grassy area between the garage and the house to admire the lay of the land. Beautiful situation. A fifty-yard back lawn, thirty yards between me and asshole O'Reilly, a shared fence with brother Williams, an assessed three hundred thousand dollar dream house in Beverly Shores.

The twins had access to better educational facilities and Yvonne was enthralled.

"Paul, aren't you glad we moved out of Hyde Park?"

"I don't know, it didn't seem like such a bad place to be."

"Maybe you don't pay attention to statistics as much as you should. Crime has come to Hyde Park, believe me."

It was a beautiful house, with beautiful grounds around it, no doubt about it. And with the large numbers of policemen, civil servants and governmental types in the area, crime, drugs and malevolent stuff was practically nonexistent.

Racial hostility was alive, but unpopular. The Irish/Italian/Jewish/Anglo majority had discovered it was expedient to mask their prejudices because there was nowhere else for them to flee.

They had watched earlier white flights leave the "inner city" to poor people of color. And some not so poor.

33

The Beverly Shores Community Club was responsible for stabilizing the community at a 60% white, 40% "ethnic" level. Their motto was "Good neighbors co-exist peacefully in expressions. We do not tolerate racism, black or white, in Beverly Shores." What that really meant is that the community was armed, but not openly fighting.

Paul Vernon sprawled on his back porch steps, briefcase leaning against the banister, his mind slowly releasing the day's tensions.

It wasn't a piece of cake to be the guy responsible for promotion of product/minority consumer development division. No one seemed to know what to do without his input.

"Uhh, Paul, now I don't want you to get offended by this or anything, but I'm lookin' at an ad that pumps up the idea of the black guy's sexual prowess. You know, sort of a sexual look at things from the minority perspective. Whaddaya think?"

"Paul, Windover wants to see you. He's real concerned about this Mexican group complaining about the new ad. Imagine, a fuckin' bunch of migrants getting pissed about anything..."

"Paul, you wanna come out to the house this weekend? I'm inviting a few of the 'in' people for barbecue 'n cocktails." God, what a crock of shit to have to deal with a bunch of pseudo liberals who thought they were unprejudiced. It was better to come home to Asshole O'Reilly and the others who clearly disliked other races and colors and made few bones about it.

He slashed away from the steps to turn the lawn sprinkler on. Damn kids. You give 'em green grass, a beautiful home, good food, fine clothes, every fucking thing you didn't have, and they won't even turn the lawn sprinkler on.

He checked his Jager-La Culture: 6:15 p.m. Tatiana was

34

at ballet and Ralph was at soccer practice. Or was he taking his chess more seriously? He slumped back onto the steps, disregarding the harm it might be doing to his Armani suit. Fuckin' kids got it made and they won't even water the grass.

Wonder what they would feel like if they had spent a few years in Chitlin Switch, back in the "old days?" Back when people didn't have shit and had to make do with whatever they had.

"It's gotta be cotton, boy, that's the crop you gotta plant." Granddad Vernon's voice pierced the veil of his daydreams.

"Raise somethin' worthwhile on your land, Paul. Don't jes' grow grass 'n cut it ever' Satiday like the rest o' them dummies. Grow somethin' you can use. Grow cotton, boy. That's the best crop in the world to have."

"Paul?! Paul?!"

He turned to stare up into his wife's face beyond the screened-in porch.

"Are you going to sit out there all evening or are you going to come in here and kiss me?"

He stumbled up the stairs with a smile on his face. After twelve years of ups 'n downs it was still a pleasure to come home to Yvonne.

"Hi, baby, what's happenin'?"

They embraced and held each other around the waist as they leaned their pelvises into each other. Fantastic looking African-Indian woman.

"We don't want to overplay the Indian thang. You know how it used to be, that everybody's grandmother was an Indian princess. Well, my grandmother Martha *was* an Indian princess."

He stared lovingly into her deep set black eyes, studied the high bridged cheeks, gently kissed the bow lined lips.

"Well, the children are at their classes and we're having

35

boneless breasts of chicken and rice, if you want something to eat."

She gently swayed her pelvis against his and subconsciously rimmed her lips with a lascivious red tongue.

"Why don't we get to the chicken 'n rice later?"

She linked her little finger into his and slowly led him upstairs to their bedroom.

"Think you might like a glass of wine before dinner?"

"Sounds like a perfect aperitif to me."

After twelve years of marriage Paul still felt excited by Yvonne's presence, her often unconventional approaches to commonplace things.

"Fuck 'em, Paul. We'll send 'em twenty-five dollars a month for the next twenty years and then run out on 'em."

And yet there were other times/situations that found her behaving as conventionally as any middle-class woman in her economic bracket could behave.

"Paul, do you really think you ought to be sitting on the front steps with a can of beer? What will our neighbors think?"

They were "personal lovers," as she defined it, and loved loving each other. The sole prerequisite for her eroticism was that the children had to be away for her to really "get free," as she put it.

The children were at classes, the liebfraumilch was chilled.

"Looks like you've had a hard day. Think you might like a hot bath and a massage?"

They traded erotic smiles as he shed his "business uniform." Beautiful sister. She knew how to come home from her own business and take care of her man. Paul slipped into the hot tub of bubble bathed water, a goblet of chilled liebfraumilch in hand. Yeahhh, this is it . . .

"A Love Supreme," one of their favorite John Coltrane albums, spilled out of the system. Yvonne was on it. She

36

knew what he loved. He soaked himself leisurely, indulgently scratching his pubic hairs, splashing hot water onto his chest. The subtle aroma of "Yoruba Lady" drifted into the bathroom...mmmmmmmm...

"Paul, you wanna massage, or are you gonna waterlog yourself?"

He responded to her invitation by popping out of the tub and drying himself with one of their huge towels.

"When I dry *my* ass, I want *my* ass dried."

He strolled into the bedroom, conveniently designed off of the master bedroom, a giant bath towel saronged around his waist.

Yvonne stood naked in a shaft of sunlight. Was it still daytime? A bottle of liebfraumilch in one hand, a jar of aloe vera in the other hand.

Beautiful Black woman, physically, psychologically, historically. He studied her face, her breasts, her stomach, her thighs, her attitude. She was there to excite, please, excite and satisfy him. She was his lover and he felt no temptation to make mistakes.

"Paul, I got all the pussy you'll ever need, just let me give it to you at my own speed, okay?"

They had been married twelve years, had twins, a boy and a girl, and he had only been tempted to commit adultery once.

Yvonne's massages were designed to quiet his nerves and arouse his libido. She did her work extremely well.

He felt the tension ease out of his hips, the tension pulse away from his shoulders, his dick harden, the work day forgotten.

"Turn over."

He sprawled on his back, trying to be tense. She played with his dick in both of her hands, as though she were playing pattycake with a cylinder, and when it stiffened to a hardened stick, she plunged it into her mouth and began to suck on

37

it like a peppermint stick.

They had a sex act. They referred to it in that way, privately...''our sex act.'' They took a certain kind of pride in being erotic with each other. He knew he could excite her day when he called from the office to say, ''yo' pussy sho did taste good to me last night, Yvonne. When you gon' gimme another lick of it?''

''What would people think of us if they saw us behaving like this?''

''I don't give a damn what the O'Reillys would think, but I'll bet you a fat man that brother Melvin and sister Lucille wouldn't say shit.''

They sprawled out beside each other on the giant sized round bed, languid, gently stroking each other's body.

''Yvonne, there's something we have to talk about.''

''What could it possibly be, after what we've just done?'' She looked at him with a dreamy smile.

They caressed and hugged each other. It was so great to have the children out of the picture for a few hours.

''It's May, and this is the second year we've been in this house, Beverly Shores...''

He felt her hand stiffen as it moved across his right thigh. ''So?''

''Yvonne, it's time for us to start planting our crop.''

Yvonne reached over into the bucket filled with ice, pulled the bottle of liebfraumilch out and took a hefty swig. She was a surprisingly earthy woman, at times.

''Paul, are you out of your mind?''

''I don't hardly think that I am.''

''Well, I do. You're talking about planting cotton in your back yard, in Beverly Shores?''

Paul Vernon slid out of bed, raced to a nearby file cabinet, pulled out an official looking document and sprawled back across the bed to read it. The print was so large he didn't need his glasses.

"The undersigned forthwith agrees to the following terms..."

He deliberately mumbled through a couple paragraphs of legalese...

"...and, in order to receive the second and final grant of $25,000.00, Paul and Yvonne Vernon do hereby agree to the following: that they willingly agree to plant, harvest, gin and create viable product from said product, namely, cotton..."

Yvonne turned onto her back, groaning.

"Ohhh nooooo, Paul. Are you going to take this shit seriously?"

"It doesn't matter whether or not I take this shit seriously or not, this is what we signed our Marcus Garveys to. We agreed to plant six to eight rows of cotton on any land we purchased (with the initial payment of $25,000.00) in the second year of our purchase and to follow the other terms. We signed an agreement and I feel duty bound to honor 'the terms.'"

"But, Paul, look, I can respect the terms 'n all that too, but let's face it, the man was senile when his will was written."

"We weren't senile when we accepted the terms."

Melvin Williams quizzed Paul Vernon about his subcontracting a guy to plow up his back yard.

"Hey, Paul! What's the deal, man? Ya trying to turn your back lawn into a cornfield?"

Paul didn't feel confident enough to tell his next door neighbor that he was having his back lawn plowed up to plant cotton in.

"Oh, I just thought I'd get the dirt turned up a bit."

The second year—the showdown year. Paul stepped off

the aisles between the rows. He felt real weird, seeding cotton.

The O'Reillys spent hours peering through their blinds at the neat rows.

"Whaddaya make of it, Peg?"

"Potatoes?"

"Are you pullin' my leg or what?"

Family opposition intensified...

"Paul, we've got to talk about this while these plants are still young enough to pull up—and out!"

"Yvonne, there's nothing to talk about. You know the terms of the will as well as I do."

"Awww, c'mon, man, that old guy was half nuts and senile at the end. No disrespect intended."

"I know all about that, but a deal is a deal. It's part of the contract we signed to get the first half of the fifty thousand dollars, remember? The money that helped us get this house."

"But, Paul, think about our neighbors, our friends. Tatiana told me that some of her girlfriends have started calling her 'Little Miss Sharecropper.' And Lois asked me the other day, 'How're things down on the plantation?' Think..."

"Think about twenty-five thousand dollars. Oh, speaking of twenty-five thousand dollars, are you aware that the short, baldheaded white guy sneaking around here last Sunday, taking pictures over the back fence, was from Greenberg, Shafton and Weiss?"

"The law firm? Are you putting me on?"

"I kid you not, my lady. Either we do what the terms call for or we'll forfeit twenty-five thousand dollars to Granddad's favorite charity."

"The Cotton Growers Association of lower Biloxi?"

"I think that's what it's called."

The Beverly Shores Community Club, responding to

40

pressure from a Black anti-cotton faction, sent one of their most diplomatic members over to have a chat with Mr. Vernon.

"Mr. Vernon, as you know, the Beverly Shores Community Club is doing everything possible to keep Beverly Shores safe from crime, maintain a high standard of life and deal with community issues..."

"Mr. Lopez, my cotton field is not a community issue."

The most diplomatic member was forced to report that he was unable to budge Mr. Vernon.

"The guy has us over a barrel, there's nothing on our books that says he can't plant cotton."

They finally took a let's-see-what-will-develop attitude like that crazy Irishman was doing a couple years ago.

"Mr. Lopez, please refrain from referring to people in our community as 'crazy Irishmen.'"

The cotton patch became a cocktail item to discuss at the Black backyard barbecues. The factions were evenly divided.

"Now, c'mon, Paul, give us a break. You know the stereotypes as well as anyone, this falls right in with jig-dancing, watermelon eating and all the rest of that crap."

Paul Vernon became self-righteously defensive.

"Now, just a minute! You guys are my neighbors, not my keepers. If I want to plant and grow cotton on my land, I'm going to grow me some cotton."

"I support the brother's position one hundred percent. I think it's a wonderful idea... So, uhhh, picturesque 'n all."

"What next? An outhouse, a watermelon patch?"

The African-Americans who were anti-cotton couldn't quite put their finger on why they found his cotton growing offensive, it just made them feel uneasy.

Meanwhile, like Topsy, the cotton just grew...and demanded lots of attention.

41

"Okay, Ralph and Tatiana, it's time for you youngsters to find out about real work. We need a coupla good weeders."

"Awwww, Dad, I don't wanna..."

"Boy, don't tell me you don't wanna do this or that, you take your behind out there and start pulling weeds like I showed you!"

Ralph and Tatiana went on strike for higher wages and a union after an hour.

"Remember?! That's what you've been teaching us, Dad. 'A labor force is only as good as its union.' "

Yvonne mediated the strike (gently siding with the strikers) and forced Paul into a position he couldn't negotiate.

"I don't think $2.50 an hour is too much to pay those babies, struggling out there in that blistering sun. And a lunch break after a half hour doesn't seem unreasonable either."

"Why don't I just go somewhere and get a couple slaves? Then I wouldn't have to be bothered by stuff like this."

By late July the cotton bolls were bursting open. Yvonne had to admit that it was a bit exciting and that the bolls were rather pretty.

"They're fleecy, like clouds."

The O'Reillys spent hours holding their sides, bursting with laughter, for awhile.

"Peg, darlin', would you believe it?! A Black guy plants a cotton field in his back yard?! Have ya ever seen anything so funny in all ya born days?!"

"I don't know, remember my Uncle Sean? He had a front yard fulla potatoes."

"But that was back in Killarney."

"Killarney, Beverly, food is food."

Ralph and Tatiana began to take some pride in their work.

"Rows one and two, my rows, are really weed free."

"You're not gonna use any pesticides, are you, Dad?"

"No, sweetheart, this will be naturally grown cotton."

The whole family stared out the side windows of the house; wandered in and out of the back porch during the course of their first summer thundershower.

"Paul, what's going to happen out there if this rain continues?"

"Well, I tell ya, Scarlett. If this keeps up the crop'll be ruined and we'll have to throw the sharecroppers out of the south forty."

"Awww, c'mon, be serious."

"I am serious. It'll mean that all this hard work was in vain. And frankly, my dear, I do give a damn."

Fortunately, the rain stopped short of washing the plants out, and the boll weevil, hearing about this patch of cotton deep in Chicago much too late, never posed a threat.

It was mid August and time to pick the cotton. The sun was blazing and the humidity was high.

"Okay, kids, be careful and be sure and get all of it. This is the weekend that you guys can say you earned your title: Cottonpickers Extraordinare."

Yvonne prepared their favorite chicken salad lunch and prowled around the house, thumbing through old magazines.

She made her appearance in her favorite Jamaican straw hat, designer jeans and brown suede gloves.

"Well, here I am. Where do I start?"

Friends called in the evening.

"Yvonne, this is Lois... Look, I drove past a few minutes ago and you guys looked like a regular bunch of sharecroppers. Any chance you'd like to farm one of the kids out for a day? Hah hah hah..."

"Paul? Mel here. Say, looka here ol' buddy, how's the pickin' goin'?"

By Sunday evening the crop was in. They had forty pounds

43

of cotton.

"Not bad, huh? For a first crop?"

Paul shipped the batch of precious white stuff to a cotton gin in Mississippi, owned by an old white man who expressed delight with the idea of ginning cotton for Northern Blacks.

"Uhh, Mr. Vernon, any mo' o' yo' folks needin' t' have they cotton ginned? Jist lemme know. Jin's Ginning Operation is always available."

They took the freshly deseeded cotton to an old Irish lady in Beverly Shores for carding and weaving.

"Mrs. O'Leary's Shoppe."

"My, my, my! What a lovely cotton! Wherever in the world did you get it?"

"We grew it in the back yard."

Mrs. O'Leary, chuckling and spinning like a mysterious faery, created four beautiful sweaters with the yarn, asked for a pound for her own use and inspired the Vernons with new pride.

"Look, we're gonna celebrate Kwanzaa this year. I think we oughta pay more attention to our roots."

Yvonne did a cost factor estimate and determined that the total cost for winding up with four sweaters was $2,500.00.

"Yeahhh, but we're the winners because the remaining twenty-five thousand dollars came in the mail today. I'd call it a nice payoff on an excellent investment."

The Vernons became minor league celebrities for a moment.

"Mr. and Mrs. Vernon, what made you do it?"

"Well, uhhh, I'd have to say it had something to do with giving our children an education."

"Your children? Education?"

It was 11:45 p.m.—fifteen minutes from the beginning of a New Year. Ralph and Tatiana were sleeping.

Paul and Yvonne, dressed in their sharpest silk pajamas, hot pink for her, red and black for him, sprawled out in front of a softly glowing fire in their living room fireplace.

The champagne bucket held a bottle three-fourths empty and a full one waiting to be opened. The hors d'oeuvres tray was filled with Yvonne's creations: tiny hamburgerettes, bite-sized shrimp sandwiches, chicken salad on tiny squares of wheat toast, Brazilian pao de queso.

Paul snuggled his head in Yvonne's lap, sipping champagne, feeling effervescent, mellow.

"Baby, you know, I've been thinking...it might be kinda nice to give the children a real chance to see where milk comes from; to have them taste vegetables that don't come off of supermarket produce stands..."

"Paul, are you talking about buying a farm?"

"Well, maybe I am, maybe I am. We raised a helluva lot more than cotton this year, you know?

"I think we had our consciousness raised with that cotton."

"I'm not going to disagree with that." She leaned over to plant a succulent kiss on his lips. "But may I suggest, before we buy the farm, let's see if we can get the horse out of the barn...mmmm?"

"Love Time"

Charley Prescott, better known as "Chuckie Baby" to the millions who watched "LoveTime," slouched in his chair, sipped imported water and wished he could blot out the sound and sight of the meeting in progress.

"'Chuckie Baby'!? Are you paying attention here?! This one show could do more to raise our ratings than anything we've ever done. Are you paying atten-shun?!"

What a brassy, crude sounding voice this woman has. Joan Rivers sounded like velvet in comparison.

"Yes, Barb, of course I'm paying attention. Don't you think I know what's at stake?"

The executive producer of *LoveTime* glared at him for a moment, and then glared at the trio of executives seated around her conference table.

Barbara I. Stone disliked Charley Prescott, aka "Chuckie Baby," the charismatic host of one of the top rated "Love

Match'' shows on television.

She disliked his white Billie Dee Williams look, the bold chin, dreamy blue eyes, the wide shoulders and slender hips, the emptiness of his attitude. Aside from the fact that he was ten years her junior.

But she was forced to concede that there was something in his chemistry that made him the perfect host for *LoveTime.*

Maybe it's because he's such a perfect reflection of the fluff-brains who come on the show, and the goofy creeps who watch it.

LoveTime was a televised version of busybody matchmaking. The couples were matched by audience vote (or so they thought) and given one all-expenses-paid date to determine their compatibility.

The critique-discussion of what happened during the date, the following program day, was the linchpin of the show.

LoveTime was slipping from the top five in its category and this meeting, the third and final one, was called to deal with the one sure way to jack it back up into the top five.

Barbara I. (''Icicle'') Stone was the executive producer of *LoveTime* and never allowed anyone to forget it.

''Okay, dudes, don't just sit there with your thumbs stuck us your asses. What do you think?!''

The trio of associate producers, yes-men from way back, exchanged hesitant glances.

No one wanted to be the first to express an opinion about anything. They were well programmed for consensus.

''Well?'' She ground the word out, speaking to the distinguished looking gray-bearded gentleman on her right.

''Well, what do you think, Morrie? Seems that I can remember you having a pair, if we go back far enough.''

Morris Steinberg shuffled his shoulders uncomfortably. This bitch. She *would* have to pick on me.

''Uhhh, do you think we've explored the...uhhh...

47

demographics of this matter closely enough?''

I. Stone's glare intensified.

"Demographics my ass! Your so-called demographics are just a fuckin' bunch of guesswork.

"I'd rather depend on astrological charts. What about it, Phil? Hiding behind your sophisticated expression again?!''

"No, not really, Barb. It's just that I think it's such an unusual piece of business, you know what I mean? We have to be concerned about our sponsors. That's what I'm most concerned about, our sponsors.''

The executive producer frowned, made a few lightning notes on the memo pad in front of her and turned to point her ballpoint at the last member of the trio as though it were a rapier.

"Brad, you're the last hickey, what do you say?''

Brad Windsor, a plastic surgeon's version of Johnny Carson, fidgeted with his late model tie.

"Well, Barbara, I've gotta agree with Morrie and Phil, to some extent. I mean, it's not like I disagree with your idea of having an interracial couple on the show for the first time.

"Oh no, it's not that at all. I tend to think that the eventual effect will be well worth the effort.''

"Get to the point, what about the sponsors?''

"The point is, I'm not so sure they'll take to the idea. They might not see it your way.''

"And why shouldn't they see it my way; because I'm a woman?''

"Chuckie Baby'' stifled a sarcastic smile, watching the trio pull their heads into their necks like beleaguered turtles. Or chickens who knew they were about to be plucked.

Brad Windsor, the boldest of the timid trio, made a small squawking sound before he found his voice.

"Ugghhh...Barb, look, I'll give you my honest

48

opinion..."

She crossed her arms over her decidedly full breasts and rolled her eyes to the ceiling.

"I think this idea of the first interracial date on *LoveTime* is a helluvan idea. I really do. My greatest concern is whether or not 'Chuckie Baby' over there, smirking at us three chicken-livered cowards, can make it work."

Barbara I. Stone turned to Charley Prescott. "Well, how about it, lover boy?"

Charley Prescott trained his most charming "Chuckie Baby" smile on the quartet.

"Let the games begin."

Stone bit her bottom lip to keep from making an obscene remark, but she couldn't prevent the thought from moving through her skull...

You airbrained butthead...

"Okay, that's it. If 'Chuckie Baby' feels he can handle the situation, then the situation is well in hand. Let's start the screen out."

Morris Steinberg shivered involuntarily. The "screen out" was his territory.

"Uhhh, Barb, just one question. What're we lookin' for here?"

"We're looking for a man and a woman, fartbrain! What else?!"

Steinberg cringed in unison with his colleagues. The woman was so crude, so basically insensitive. "I mean..."

"Yeah, yeah, I know what you mean. It's going to be a white man and a Black woman, okay? Y'all got that? A white fuckin' man and a Black fuckin' woman!"

Her hard gray eyes darted from one to the other. "Awright a'ready, let's get the lead out! Move it!"

"Barb?"

Brad Windsor straightened his tie nervously.

"Yeah, what is it, Brad? I've got another meeting in ten minutes."

"What's the time frame here?"

"Good question, for a change. We're talking about two weeks from today."

The trio stared at her as though they had been given a collective slap in the face.

Morris Steinberg recovered first.

"That doesn't give us a lot of time, does it?"

"No, it doesn't, now get busy!"

The men shuffled out with as much dignity as they could muster. "Chuckie Baby" trailed the trio with a smirk on his handsome face.

"Chuck, wait a sec, I want a word with you."

Prescott held back a giveaway frown. "Wait a sec" could mean anything. On two occasions it was attempted seduction. Sexual harassment?

He flashed her his neutral "Chuckie Baby" smile.

"Yeah, Barb, what is it?"

"I just thought I'd feel you out about this, you know—key in on your private feelings."

He made a couple quick mental calculations and came up with confused sums. You could never predict what Barbara "Icicle" Stone was about.

"My private...feelings?"

"Sure, you know the success of this thing depends on you."

"Let the games begin."

Stone's eyes walled back into her upper lids with exasperation.

"You already said that, 'Chuckie Baby,' remember?"

"Oh, so I did."

"What I'm trying to find out is whether or not you feel that you can handle an interracial dating situation in front

50

of millions of bigoted, biased, prejudiced assholes. We're apt to have everybody, from the Klan to the African Daughters of the American Revolution, on our tails.''

Charley Prescott gave the question a thoughtful thirty seconds, causing Stone's teeth to grind with impatience.

"Yeahhh, yeah, I think I can handle it.''

"Good. That's all I wanted to know.''

She abruptly terminated their conversation by jerking the door open.

"See ya later, 'Chuckie Baby.' ''

The following days witnessed more feverish activity than usual in the triple-decked offices of Barbara I. Stone.

Morris Steinberg, the "screen out" man, frantically set his computers for the right Black woman who would be willing to date a white guy, and talk about the experience on network TV.

The applicants were few and mostly unacceptable for one reason or another.

"Hey, Morrie, did you know that the Carter woman was on parole for killing her husband? Oh, incidentally, he was a white guy.''

The problem finding a white man who was ready, willing and wanting a date with a Black woman was less difficult.

"Okay, we've narrowed it down to ten, let's pick one.''

The show was three days away from air time before they were able to create the appropriate match up, almost.

Barbara I. Stone raged over the snail's pace.

"What the hell is it with you fishheads?! My God! You mean to tell me you can't find a Black woman and white guy who want to be on television together? Out of a population of millions?! I don't fuckin' believe this!''

"Barb?''

"I see mixed couples walking the streets every day. I see them everywhere I go.''

51

"Barbara?"

"I see them in restaurants, movie houses, churches, laundromats, every fuckin' place, f' God's sake!"

"Barbara?"

"Well, spit it out, Morrie, don't just stand there digging in your crack."

"We have a couple."

"Why the hell didn't you say so?! I was beginning to think that I'd have to get out there and find a couple myself."

Wanda Tyson and Jeffrey Nelson were invited to the offices of Barbara I. Stone Enterprises, Inc. for a preshow briefing by the associate producers of *LoveTime*.

They seemed to be ideally matched for the experiment. She was a junior college science teacher and he was the owner of a small computer repair firm.

They were both attractive in a wholesome, toothy sort of way, but fell short of being handsome or gorgeous.

Brad Windsor adjusted his tie for the tenth time.

"Now then, we don't want to have a lot of ethnic stuff cluttering things up, you know what I mean? We just sorta want people, anybody channeling in, to imagine themselves in your place.

"Of course, they're going to see that you're white and she's black."

"African-American!"

"Right! But we don't want you to identify yourselves in that way. You know what I mean?"

Despite the efforts made to keep the interracial show a secret, a few sponsors backed off. 1990's.

"Sorry, Barb, cancel us for this one. It's the kind of headache we don't need."

Charley Prescott spent an extra hour at the spa, the day before the show, calming his nerves. He wasn't unduly anxious about the upcoming historical event.

52

I'll just be myself. After all, how many Chuckie Babys do they have?

He sprawled back in the hot tub, arms spread ecstatically around the rim, carefully avoiding the bold eyes of the weight-lifting blonde woman and the dark-eyed homosexual vamp across from him.

The afternoon of the first interracial date on *LoveTime* was fed heaping spoons of anxiety by all concerned parties.

"Where the hell are these people?!"

"They're on their way to the studio, Ms. Stone."

"What's the audience look like?"

"We kicked a few neo-Nazi types out..."

"The racial makeup?"

"Kinda quirky: About sixty-five percent white, male and female, lots of Black chicks..."

"No Black men?"

"A few, maybe more."

Barbara I. Stone paced back and forth in the control booth as usual, giving the director of *LoveTime* last minute directions.

"If there's a hint of a disturbance in the audience I want you to go to a commercial immediately. Got that?! Immediately! I don't want to have to edit any more tape than necessary."

Tom Downey, Jr., nodded dutifully. He was almost immune to Stone's crazed behavior after three months of directing *LoveTime under* her direction.

The credits rolled, the theme music played and "Chuckie Baby" danced down the five steps, stage left.

The fix was on, two Black males were going to be shown on the video-interview insert and then Jeffrey Nelson. The audience response registers were monitored to award the date to Jeffrey Nelson, no matter what.

The studio audience made a collective gasp when Jeffrey Nelson appeared on the screen talking about what he expected from a date.

"I feel really turned off by a woman who uses a toothpick. Or drinks beer out of a can."

"Chuckie Baby" conducted the onstage in-studio interview in his usual suave fashion.

"Now then, Miss Wanda Tyson, what you're saying is that a man doesn't have to make an effort to impress you?"

"Exactly. I'm the kind of woman who really understands and appreciates what a man has to go through in life. Why should I add to his problems by being a problem?"

The moment of truth only lasted for the length of one commercial. There was a longer gasp that deteriorated into a ghastly moan when Wanda Tyson announced that she had chosen Jeffrey Nelson over the two African-American men.

The telephones began to ring immediately, voicing outrage, delight, indignation, pleasure, confusion, racism, altruism, fear.

Barbara I. Stone paced back and forth in her office, smacking her left fist into her right palm.

"Dammit! Why didn't I think of this before?"

The overwhelming evidence of the African-American repugnance of the sister's choice was registered from one end of the class spectrum to the other.

"I mean, hey, don't get me wrong, man. Anybody oughta be able to do they thang with whoever they want to, you know what I mean? But if we got a Black sister who's so screwed up that she chooses a white boy over two brothers, I don't even wanna hear about it, let alone see it."

The white reaction spanned the same spectrum.

"So, the dude wants to date a jungle bunny. Who gives a shit?"

LoveTime was the topic of conversation.

"What do you think they're really saying by doing this?"

Wanda Tyson and Jeffrey Nelson kept their date. And where they went and what they did was a Stone secret.

Morris Steinberg, Phil Flint and Brad Windsor spent most of the "date night" telephoning each other, trying to dig out clues.

"What do you think is going to happen?"

"If the damn thing doesn't boost our ratings, Barbara Bitch is going to torture us to death."

"That's a pretty radical scenario, Morrie, don't you think?"

"Chuckie Baby" smiled his way past a clot of middle-aged political activists on his way into the studio.

They were protesting something but he felt too pressured to read the placards; find out what they were protesting for or against.

People are always protesting something or other. They should try to figure out a better way to spend their time.

Rushing from makeup and into a punchy five minute war talk with Barbara I. Stone didn't give him a lot of time to fix on preshow jitters.

"Now, just remember, Chuck, we want you to treat these people just like any other couple, got it?"

"Sure, Barb, no problem. I got us through the first part okay, didn't I?"

"You did okay, okay? It could've been smoother. Just remember what I said."

The credits rolled, the theme music played and "Chuckie Baby" danced down the five steps, stage left.

"And now, ladies and gentlemen, without further ado, let's find out what happened last night," he spoke into the teeth of the audience's applause.

"Once again, Wanda Tyson and Jeffrey Nelson, the

winnahs of yesterday's *LoveTime* date fare of two hundred dollars. Let's bring them out here and get the story fresh from the horses' mouths.''

Stone winced. How many times have I told that jerk not to say that?

The couple entered from stage right (no steps for them to dance down), took their places on the extended love seat, center stage.

"Chuckie Baby" placed himself in the middle, flashing his charming "Chuckie Baby" smile to both sides.

"Now then, who wants to start? How 'bout you, Wanda?

"What? When? Where? How many?"

He gave his usual pseudo-lascivious offside wink to the studio audience. Morris Steinberg called Barbara I. Stone in the control booth.

"We have reports of people sitting in front of TV sets in bunches. Looks like we've come up with a winner!"

"You're damned right *I've* come up with a winner, pal."

She slammed the phone back into its cradle and refocused on the show. They were fading back in after the first commercial break.

"And then what happened?"

"We talked on the phone after the show, you know, to get to know each other a little better before our date."

"And what did you talk about?"

Another lascivious smirk into the camera.

"Well, the only thing he really seemed to be interested in was my sex life: Had I made it with other guys, how many? That sort of thing."

"Chuckie Baby" swallowed hard and fast, made a Brad Windsor tie adjustment.

"And just why do you think he was interested in your...uh...previous sex life?"

"I don't know why, to be frank, but I've found that's a

56

fairly common trait in some guys, you know?"

Barbara I. Stone placed both fists on her narrow hips and leaned closer to peer into the television monitors.

What the hell is going on here?

Jeffrey Nelson frowned as though a confidence had been betrayed.

"Awww, c'mon, Wanda, you're twenty-four years old. How many twenty-four-year-olds do you know who are still virgins?"

Raucous laughter and baboon whoops echoed through the television studio. It was obvious that they had not hit it off too well. Stone had to answer the telephone three times in as many minutes.

The word was out, the show was "happening." "Chuckie Baby" was fighting a derailment of the *LoveTime* format.

"So, you drove over to pick 'er up?"

"No, we made arrangements to meet at this beachside restaurant."

"He didn't want to pick me up because he was afraid of the neighborhood I live in."

"Chuckie Baby" felt perspiration dampen his armpits. What's the deal with you two assholes? Don't you remember the ground rules? This is the *LoveTime* show, not "Fightin' Words."

He could imagine the gripping look of anger on Stone's face in the control booth.

"Awright, so you met in this seaside restaurant. You had an excellent seafood dinner?"

"We had a seafood dinner, but it wasn't all that great. It was sorta spoiled by this dress she was wearing. It was so bright it was almost blinding."

"I think my kente cloth was a lot more stylish than that plaid horse blanket sports coat you were wearing."

They were snarling at each other now, the hostility slicing

57

back and forth. "Chuckie Baby" winked into the camera, mugged for the studio audience, indicating that this hostility was a part of the act.

"After dinner, what then?"

He took surprised note of the audience reaction. They seemed to be enjoying the whole thing.

"We had a big argument about whether or not we were going to go dancing or to a movie."

"I knew I wasn't going to go dancing with a man in a plaid horse blanket and white socks.

"Did I mention that? That he was wearing white socks?"

"Chuckie Baby" mugged a little harder; made a stronger effort to cool the hostility level down.

The *LoveTime* couple, Wanda Tyson and Jeffrey Nelson, weren't buying into his labor.

"We compromised and went to the movies."

"What did you see?"

"He insisted, for some strange reason, that we go to see this ol' Spike Lee thing."

"I thought she'd enjoy it, Chuck, it seemed like it would be her kind of movie."

"What made you think that? I've never liked any of his stupid movies."

"Ahem, so you went to the movies and you didn't enjoy..."

"I thought it was a great movie, she didn't like it."

"There's no doubt in my mind why you liked it," Wanda Tyson almost screamed across "Chuckie Baby."

"Back in a moment, folks, after these important words from our sponsors."

Phones rang, tempers flared, people hollered and screamed at each other; Barbara I. Stone's eyes glittered with a strange light. *LoveTime*'s ratings shot up to the top three.

"Chuckie Baby" literally had to pry the couple's hands

from each other's throats at the end of their segment of the show. Like a circus animal trainer, he made his announcement.

"As you can see...now, now, Wanda! Ladies and gentle...no punches Jeffrey! No punches please... Ladies and gentlemen, sometimes the course of a date does not a true course run. Now, then, without further ado, let's go onto couple number two."

By prior arrangement, Morris Steinberg, Phil Flint and Brad Windsor raced to Barbara I. Stone's office immediately after the program ended.

She met them with her usual brand of humor. "Good. For once, constipation didn't hold you bastards up. Well, give it to me! Whaddaya think?"

The trio immediately went into their low profile mode, casting surreptitious glances at each other.

"You don't have to waffle! It's a fuckin' hit! We got a whole new fuckin' ballgame for *LoveTime* to play."

The men applauded irrationally, off tempo, crazily, puzzled.

"Okay, listen up, you crumbums! We're onto something here. We're going to be known as the show where you can have a date with someone you'd never have anything to do with, let alone date."

The trio exchanged eye signals.

What the hell is she talking about?

What do you think she's talking about?

I don't know.

"Cut the eye drama and give *me* your undivided attention. I want you to find me a youthful looking concentration camp survivor—male or female—and an unrepentant Nazi. They tell me they got lots of 'em in Argentina and northeastern Brazil. We may have to go to Bavaria, who knows? Get my drift?"

59

Morris Steinberg's eyes walled back into their sockets as though he was feeling a knife plunge into his back.

"And we'll go from there—battered women dating rapists, rapists dating virgins, ex-priests and nuns who've become prostitutes—the works. Any questions?"

"Chuckie Baby" slouched in his seat, gulping swallows of Jack Daniels as he absorbed the Stone's commitment to trash.

"Okay, so this guy looks like the 'Elephant Man's' little brother and the woman is the winner of the Sioux City, Iowa, 'Miss Cornshucks' contest.

"Anybody have an idea where we can find the ugliest bastard in the Middle West? That's our next show. Wake up you pootbutts! We're gonna be number one in our class. Let's git busy!"

The trio shuffled out, heads down. Stone grabbed Chuckie Baby's coat as he shuffled out behind the trio.

"Chuckie, stay a sec."

He stood in place, sucking on his drink, a dead look on his face.

"Yeah, Barb, what is it?"

"It's gonna git rough out there, think you can hang in there?"

He stared into her glittering eyes, took note of the cruel lines crescenting her lips, felt the urge to spit in her face.

"Let the games begin," he spoke slowly, carefully.

"Good, glad to hear that."

LoveTime became one of the most popular shows of its type, for all time, and "Chuckie Baby" was known for his opening line.

"Let the games begin."

The Survival Tango
(for BaBa Mike Cook)

In Los Angeles they live in garages, "backhouses," overturned Kleenex boxes, in the off brand room of sympathetic friends, in their cars (if they have one), in other folks' cars, in the park, at the beach.

In Chicago they stay wherever there is a bit of steamed heat, in the winter, and wherever they can find some shade and a water fountain, in the summer.

Some of them are artists (singers, dancers, actors, actresses, sculptors, photographers, contortionists, poets, distortionists, novelists), many of them are self-deceptive con men/women, jiffy tricksters, smile-awhile types, karma freaks, drunks, fiends of every type, drug and otherwise, religious fanatics, ascetics, creeps, spur of the moment victims, diced-up products of the time, some of them are artists, real people.

The two basic rhythms played for their dance, the Survival

Tango, are hot and cold, with dozens of degrees either way in between.

The individuals doing the dance have orchestrated a pattern they feel is suitable for their shape, ego size and aura. Or they seem to be trying to achieve that goal.

Inevitably, problems surface wherever these individuals attempt to do their dance movements openly. It's one thing to be undercover, another whole number to come out with it.

That's the main problem with the "Tango": It's a mostly secret dance because those who know the best steps cannot teach, and those who attempt to teach do not know the dance.

The Survival Tangos have to be absorbed, not taught. They must be lived because they cannot be bought. And besides, who wants to learn a dance with six hundred dips, fifteen hundred movements, and music that changes with each couple—or whenever the check is in the mail?

Uhh huhhh...

It would've been impossible *not* to feel the tension in the workshop after the sister finished reading her poem.

Most of the tension was directed at the poet, not the poem. Jungle madness.

"Yella bitch! Who she think she is?!"

It was 1966 and all of the African-Americans in Watts had become poets, seers, playwrights, proposal writers, critics (POST WATTS REBELLION).

"Well, I'll tell you what I think. I think the sister is fulla shit! I don't really think she knows what she's talkin' about. I can tell from the color of her skin that she's obviously one of those house nigger-booshie types who's tryin' to relate to the real deal but ain't quite gettin' there... hahhahhahhah..."

Dark-skinned African-Americans were being validated by

Madison Avenue ("Black is Beautiful") and many of them were freaking out on the attention.

"My daddy was blacker than the telephone."

We watched her struggle with more militant types out in the workshop parking lot.

"Okay, so, in your poem you say you a bad black bitch, huh? Well, let's see how bad you really are!"

We watched her, on more than one occasion, take a deep sigh, gently place her notebooks in the back seat of her ancient Volkswagen, and fist-claw-duel with crown cropped African-American women who were trying to whip every ounce of Blackfoot-Irish-Choctaw-Dutch blood out of her.

Sometimes she bled, you could tell when you saw burgundy colored tears, but those who made her bleed had to pay a price for the blood. She fought back.

Who said that there are no vegetables harvested without seeds planted?

We watched the attacks grow weaker—"Hey, I don't see shit wrong with the sister's shit?!"—and the quality of the poet's work get stronger.

"This poem will not make everyone feel more comfortable."

We listened to those who, once upon a time, discouraged her become her dance partners.

"You talkin' about DC? DC is one of the baddest motherfuckers around. I was there in the beginning, when she first started out. She was one of the baddest bitches in the workshop. Everybody dug her!"

We went from there...

It was always tricky-chancy to check her out in the white nightspots, trying to soul-perch her steatopygous body on those narrow-minded Valley high stools.

63

There were nights when it seemed that the only thing preventing her from spilling off the stool was the ethereal quality of her voice, the hipper people said, "You know, I don't go out of my way to dig but two people: DC and Melba."

They both sang in the upper registers of African Romance, which means that, even when they were singing Cole Porter standards—"I get no kick from Champagne...," they were considered too down for the lightweight cognoscenti.

A number of people in Watts (and Japan) thought that Melba was a heaven-sent figure. When she stood in front of the audience at the Watts Towers (no stool available—lack of funding) or the Osaka Jazz Appreciation Bureau, her childish speaking voice warned her listeners to listen closely because she wasn't entirely responsible for what was going to come out of her; "I asked the Father this evening to tell me, to tell me—what should I sing to these brothers 'n sisters?"

On summer hazed afternoons in Watts, and other venues south of Manchester, she left audiences feeling as though they had experienced vocal hypnotism.

"Sister be doin' it!"

And forced people north of Santa Monica Boulevard to believe in her talents.

"We've just heard an incredibly gifted artist."

"God gave me this voice to use as He commands."

She never wore her pains on her shoulders, allowed her broken heart the indulgence of mending in front of an audience, or pretended to be anyone but herself. It seems that this was the Problem. The agent wanted her to be what he wanted her to be, the wigmaker wanted her to be what she wanted her to be, the Japanese wanted her to be Japanese.

There were even rumors that some of her biggest fans wanted her to be thin.

64

She had to do a helluva dance to move through all of that, and is still doin' it. Maybe that's why her struggle continues. Tango.

We went from Here to There...

Sylvia must've been doing her dance before black pepper got its name. Her dance was the ritualized movements of Africa carried into Cuba and Puerto Rico.

Black sister, a Celia Cruz of dance.

"Curl dee bod-dy! Curl dee bod-dy!"

We went to her dance classes as though we were attending seances, or lessons in body magic.

"Watch! Do thees as I do eet! Now do eet!"

We seldom did "eet" as she did "eet," but we were privileged to see how it was done.

Her body was built to carry the rhythm of the drama. She moved from student to student as though a secret rhythm was being played especially for her.

"Sylvia, what makes a dancer?"

"Thees is a berry gud question. I would say that the dancer is someone who has a gud connection with many of the divine energies."

She was never a simple person to talk with, not able to give herself over to American style joking. Or funny stuff for the sake of being funny. But she did have a beautiful sense of sarcasm and humor.

"I ask every person to do thees moov-ment, why you are doin' someting oppo-seet?"

Sylvia was a dark-skinned African woman from Cuba who taught West African and "Latin" dances, and danced for a living. That was the problem.

We didn't understand how serious her problem was until we took a hard look behind the regal facade.

"Move your hips! Move your bod-dy! Move!"

"Look, isn't that Sylvia over there?"

The woman pointed out in the back seat of the bus looked lonely, crushed, ill at ease. We made a surreptitious study of our dance mistress.

She looked older, slumped down in the corner, lost. We pretended not to see her as she dug down into a cluttered diddy bag and pulled out a corn tortilla.

Where was she going? To her dance class, of course. We got off the bus a discreet distance behind her, watching the transformation of semi-raggedy clothes metamorph into ethnic costume, the beaten slump elevate to statuesque carriage, the shuffle of an old lady become the designer stride of a well-conditioned athlete.

She was giving last minute instructions to the drummer for the evening class when we wandered into the gymnasium.

"Clap-clap clap-clap-clap! This is eet! Thees are the rhythms I want. Unnerstand?"

We hurriedly pulled on our dancing leotards, kicked off restraining shoes.

"Hokay! Eberybody! Line up! Let us begin to do the exercises! Uh one, uh two, uh tree..."

She strode up and down the aisles of stretching bodies, pausing to push a stomach in here, pull a leg there, offer a bit of encouragement.

"Paulette, you must loose thees rubber tire around your waist band."

During the course of the warm-up exercise period, she leaned over to whisper in our ears..."I saw you on the bus today." And strode away like a general inspecting his troops. Tango.

66

Tabula

Tabula sorta snuck up on us, like she was there before we fully realized who she was. My experience with her started off with us doing a program together in the basement of a Methodist church in Echo Park, Los Angeles.

Some good hearted clergyman decided it would be a good idea for his "Hispanic" flock to be exposed to "culture." So he invited me to read a little Shakespeare, and for Tabula to do some West African dancing.

She put in an appearance with a fantastic jimbey drummer who smelled like sinsemilla bud. Little sister, about five feet tall, one hundred and two pounds (if that), and filled with West African dance movements and love.

I couldn't finish my Shakespearean number too soon, I wanted to check her out. It was a strange setting for a superior presentation of West African dancing.

The Shakespearean number had been relatively easy for

the audience to get into (it didn't take a lot for the gang members, the "vato locos," to relate to excerpts from *Romeo and Juliet* and *Othello*) but the African dance thing was something else for them.

It was ironic that they would get off into cracking stupid jokes and goofing around like monkeys, in their crummy imitation of what she was doing, but she didn't let it go on for very long.

"Now then, since you all know about this dance that I'm doing, I want the first row to come up here and do it!"

She was small, dark and as potent as a stick of dynamite.

The "vatos" chilled out immediately. No one wanted to be put on the spot.

"Now then—now that we've straightened that out, I want you all to pay attention. This is a welcoming dance that comes from Ghana. It's done by the young women of the village when a stranger is being received."

She explained movements, attitudes, clued their hard corner heads into accepting the idea that African dancing from the west coast wasn't like street fighting, or go-go-girl bumpin' 'n grindin'.

She got over. And when her presentation was over they stood and applauded. She could've been the lead dancer of the Ballets Africains.

I think we were paid ten dollars each for our participation in this cultural mishmash.

"We certainly wanna thank you guys for making this evening happen. It really means a lot, you know what I mean," saith the clergyman.

Ten lousy bucks! I watched her pay half of her ten to the drummer as they headed for the church parking lot. Ten lousy bucks for a lifetime of devotion to West African dance forms.

68

I was even more pissed off, watching her stash her dance gowns in the trunk of her fifteen-year-old car. How could so much talent be so unappreciated that she'd be paid ten dollars and be forced to ride in a fifteen-year-old car?

A few years later, I checked her out in much more lucrative circumstances. She was driving a later model car, wearing more expensive gowns and dancing better than ever.

"Yeahhh, I remember the church program very well. I hadn't had anything to eat for two days prior to the performance and I only had a cup of gas in my tank.

"I was going through what you might call 'a difficult time.' But I assumed that if I continued dancing, everything would be okay.

"That's one of the lessons that you learn from the Survival Tango. So far, so good."

Dean Dale Jackson

How many times did I drive to San Bernardino with a smile on my face, and return to L.A. frowning?

Dean Dale Jackson was always disappointing but he never disappointed. We all wished, at some point, that he *would* disappoint us and not go into an alcoholic tantrum, figure out a way to stay out of absurd situations; act right, for a change.

It never happened and we remained confused about the why of it not happening: His wife? His friends?

Talented brother. He could write a novel, a short story, an article, make a face out of porcelain, fine tune a car, but he never seemed to be able to get himself together.

"'Fuck you talkin' about, motherfucker? I am together! You the one who ain't together!''

How many drunk scenes did he play out? Hundreds? Thousands? There were times when it seemed that his life

70

was a drunk scene.

We often questioned his alcoholism.

"Dean Dale? Awwwww, that dude ain't no alky. He's fucked up but he ain't no real alky. Watch him closely. That's an act he puts on."

"C'mon, Dean Dale, cut the shit! You're only a basic fuckin' beer drinker. How can you be fucked up?!"

"How 'bout a shot of ouzo?"

The Greek ouzo helped him turn the corner on his nebulous alcoholism. Those who had earlier doubts became converts.

"Did you see that asshole piss in that flowerpot at the Meriwethers' party?"

His wife, a poor sister who had elevated herself to middle-class proud, suffered.

"Dean Dale, why don't you stop acting like an idiot-fool?!"

Weird thing about the brother is that he had not always acted like an "idiot-fool." It seemed to be a discovered sector of his psyche.

He had been, at one point, "the bright young devil" who was responsible for importing African-American activists to a white college campus for fun 'n games.

"Hey, brotherman, you wanna drive up here and read some of your awesome shit to these white folks? I'll budget a hundred dollars for you."

Stokely Carmichael came, Stanley Crouch (before he became "Stanley Crouch"), Audrey Lourde, Ojenke, Eric Priestley, Baby Blood, and a whole bunch of other folks.

From African-American radical to upstage, the status quo to a naked asshole who pissed in flowerpots took a heap of psychic energy.

"You know what Dean Dale did?"

It got to be more than his wife could deal with. She split, Peugeot packed to the gills, her brainpan sizzling.

71

"I give up. I can't figure out what's wrong with him."

He went into an awkwardly orchestrated downspin after her defection.

"When've you seen Dean Dale?"

"Haven't you heard? He's living with a young sister on welfare who's got six kids."

How many trips did we make to San Bernardino with a smile on our faces and return to L.A. frowning?

"Look, man, I'm going to put it to you straight up. Your car needs a new transmission and a tune up."

"How can you tell?"

"Shit! I can listen to the motherfucker and tell." Being mechanically inclined was like a second layer of skin for him.

"How did you learn so much about cars, Dean Dale?"

"Hey, any motherfucker growing up in the west knows about cars. I had built two of 'em from scratch before I was fifteen."

He could take a bottle of ouzo and disappear under the hood of a car for days, and when he surfaced, drunk, belligerent and speaking in tongues, the car he had been working on could levitate.

Dean Dale brought the same kind of gifted understanding to the sculptor's art. The brother could grab a piece of granite, a section of driftwood, a clump of clay, a length of metal and turn it into a sum-ie stroked bouquet of roses, the life mask of a Masai warrior, a delicately torched portrait of a swan in flight. His hands created art.

The art came from his hands, the madness came from somewhere else.

"Dean Dale," (nobody ever called him "Dean," it was always "Dean Dale") "we gotta talk, man."

"What about? You want some of this?"

"Nawww, put the ouzo bottle down for a minute, brother. Let's get serious."

72

"Fuck you, man! I am serious."

"You're not serious, you're drunk."

I don't think any of us would've cared very much if the dude hadn't been so damned talented. An elitist position was claimed for him that he never occupied or seriously responded to.

"Butler here?"

"Ain't no niggahs named Butter in here!"

"He's kinda short, dark skinned, lots of grease in his hair. His woman's name is Penelope, she's blonde with blue eyes . . ."

"Jes' tol' you we ain't got no niggahs in here. Billy Bob, there's a niggah here lookin' for some niggah named Butterball."

"Butler! His name is Butler."

"Don't get smart with me, niggah. Stay in this doorway another minute and I'm gonna blow your nappy fuckin' head into the next county."

"His name is Butler, my man. You sure you don't know a Butler . . . ?"

It could've been the opening for a fictional piece if it hadn't been true.

"Dean Dale, do you know you almost got your ass blown away back there?"

"By who? Or should I say by whom?"

Crazy shit like that. We had to stop hanging out with him for the sake of survival. He was a bad omen, an accident asking to happen, a self-destructor, his approach to everything negative.

"If you were really a writer, you'd be writing about this shit, not trying to become a part of it."

"I am writing about it, I am writing about it, but lots of it ain't reachin' the page."

Transmissions from supernatural cars fell on his head.

73

broke his arms, legs, ribs, but couldn't stop him from drinking.

"Fuck it! Why should I stop doing what I'm doing? I can still swallow, can't I?"

His way with the sculpting knife bottomed out when he fell to sleeping under a San Bernardino overpass.

"Man, how could you allow yourself to sink this low?"

"I wanted to get down into the underbelly of it all. You know what I mean?"

None of us knew what he meant, honestly, and some of us stopped trying to figure his trip out.

"Fuck Dean Dale! He ain't about shit! Here is a motherfucker who can write his ass off, knows how to build race cars from scratch and can take a blow torch and sculpt roses out of sheet metal, and he's going around talkin' some shit about the underbelly?! Underbelly my fuckin' asshole!"

The brother discovered burglary during his "underbelly" period. But he wasn't as skillful at breaking and entering as he was with writing, sculpting or fixing errant vehicles.

"Dear Brotherman, I'm doing a hard year in Chino. It's not really that bad a scene. Don't get me wrong, this is not really where I want to be but it ain't the worst place in the world.

"I think the underpass where I lived was the worst place. It was pure underbelly."

We read his letters, refused his requests for funky go-go-girl g-strings and belly dancers' bras, and gradually weaned ourselves from his behavior.

How many times did they drive to San Bernardino with smiles on their faces, and returned to L.A. frowning?

Tango misstep.

Jo Bellissima

Jo was one of the most beautifully beige people I've ever known. She was a true beige down to the bottoms of her feet, and she was beautiful to boot.

The physically beautiful side was not one of those gleaned from a magazine job. She was physically beautiful because she was a dancer, and the art had created her beauty.

How tall was she? Five-five, five-six or so. But when you looked at her from ten yards away, she seemed to be a clean cut six-footer. It had to do with the way she stood and moved.

It was a terrible beauty, because it gave the appearance of strength; the wonderfully developed limbs, the Nzingha carriage that cloaked a hugh soft spot.

This vulnerability was directly linked to two distinct traits: alcoholism and racial confusion. Jo was an Indian-African-American who felt awkward about saying that she was either one of the two.

Jo, with her beige-ness, her wavy-straight hair and her love for Italy (where she'd been given the opportunity to simply be a superb beige dancer) was an enigma.

Dancing-being an Indian-African-American-Alcoholic-being beautiful-Italy.

Those seemed to be the major links in Jo's life.

In deepest Watts, where I was first exposed to her dance classes (she was kinder and less militant than Sylvia), she taught by example. I suspect it had something to do with language.

She didn't want to be faulted for not speaking Ghettoese, so she had obviously opted for action rather than words.

She pushed and pulled a bit but mostly she danced-taught. Her dance-teaching was an exquisite exposure to Jo's special sensitivity.

She would grab the sluggish student's shoulders and rivet her attention to the motion with her head, a shimmer of the hips, a shuffle of the feet, an Attitude.

It wouldn't've been possible to say that you didn't understand or that you couldn't figure it out after she had worked with you for five minutes.

She made you understand Dance. She was clear about what that is. She wasn't clear about who she was.

"Of course, I know I have Black blood in my veins, but I feel Native American, even though I've never lived the lifestyle of a Native American. But I love Italy too, I love it as though I were an Italian."

Maybe that ambivalence is what created the alcoholic strain.

The racial indecision may have fueled the alcoholism. Who knows? The precedent for people of severely mixed racial loyalties being addicted to different stuff has been well documented (check Michael Jackson's operation out).

It would take a seasoned shrink to validate any suspicion

a layperson might have about Jo's alcoholism, but it was there.

Some evenings, after a day of teaching African-American girls how to channel their energy (they already know how to dance), she would hang out with the security guard at the Watts Towers (the brother who used to whisper to tourists, "That man didn't build these things by himself, he had help.) and sip moonshine that had been freshly made by one of the old-timers who lived across the street from the Towers.

She didn't get drunk when she drank, she didn't wobble or stumble. There wasn't really a difference in her when she was sober or when she was drunk.

And she could drink a dazzlingly huge amount of wine, gallons of it.

"I loved drinking wine in Italy." Complex woman.

Being beautiful (as defined by people who were aliens to her art, caused a few problems also) meant having men fall in love, without a trace of understanding what love was supposed to mean.

So, she suffered from the attention given her by jealous men. Some of it was brutal.

"Yes, Giovanni did beat me but you know how Italian men are."

It gave Dance a better reason to play a part in her life.

"When I'm dancing I don't feel any of the normal pressures of life. I don't feel that I have to define myself racially, I don't feel beautiful or ugly. I simply feel graceful, light, a dancer."

Finally, the dance couldn't give her the freedom she needed, she had to go back to Italy. It literally happened that suddenly.

One Saturday afternoon she was artfully instilling the feel for dance in a group of sluggards, and the following afternoon she was in Milan.

We talked about her for months and each person gave us an unthought of facet to study.

"She was obviously one of the most gifted dancers I've ever seen. I don't know about her choreographic stuff, but she was a top dancer, tops."

"She used to piss me off with those Indian headbands and kente cloth skirts. It was like watching all the confusion you needed to see in one person."

"Sister could put away some booze. I remember seeing her drink a half a mason jar of ol' man White's moonshine.

"Now you know she could drink if she could handle that moonshine."

"Wasn't she beautiful?! You know what I'm saying? She was a real beauty. I don't think I ever saw her with makeup on or with an air about her looks.

"Even with the drinking that you people talk about, all I can remember is a superbly conditioned athlete.

"She was built like a woman should be built, full up front, but not too ample behind. And carried a serious mind around in that lovely head of hers."

"I disliked her for awhile, for loving Italy so much. I just couldn't get ready for the idea of a sister that fine giving it up to the Italians. But then I had to look at it from a freedom perspective.

"Who am I to say what another person's loves and dislikes should be? I miss her. I feel like she left a hole in my life."

Jo lives on the island of Ischia now, far away from this Tango she didn't want to learn.

Impression of a Mestre

It was a cold, clear, sunny morning when Mestre Moraes made his appearance at the loft, January 27th, 1990, in Oakland, California.

Professor Themba Mashama, Capoeira Angola instructor, had the vision and sensitivity to invite Mestre Moraes, a member of a select fraternity, to the Bay Area; Capoeira Angola Mestres are not found on every street corner in Brazil.

For those of us who waited, and had never known a consecrated mestre, the vibe was semi-electric. Mestre Moraes is a practitioner of an art that was born in Africa way back in the 15th century.

He is, in a sense, the son of a vital link of our heritage, and the art he was bringing stemmed from that knowledge. He could be compared, in other terms, to a cardinal or an archbishop of our martial art.

We greeted each other warmly, but cautiously.

He gave off the impression of being someone who knew something. We saw it gleaming in his eyes.

The Capoeira Angola-life instruction class began. The first day was a blur of vivid impressions.

"You should be like a monkey to play Capoeira Angola."

He came with berimbau wisdom, pandiero knowledge, agogo rhythms, atabaque strength and the psychological capability to deal with many different psyches.

He took us straight to the heart of African-Brazil with the ginga. The ginga: that seemingly innocent dance step that contains so much maliciousness in Capoeira Angola.

We understood, after a few demonstration movements, why being a monkey would be a great aid in the play Capoeira Angola.

The pace of what was happening in the loft seemed almost glacial, in comparison to Capoeira Angola Regional classes. No muscular frenzy, no macho exhibitionism.

It was a unique experience. None of us had ever been in a class that recessed while the mestre asked, "How is your relationship to Eshu?"

Some of us gave our definition of who we thought Eshu was, some of us wondered about the nature of the question; he made all of us more aware of the importance of the Religion. And so it moved, from one movement to the next movement, each done with icy precision.

The presence, in many ways, of this African-American mestre-man (southern branch) was electrifying for some of us African-Americans (northern branch) who came, saw and were overwhelmed by his unique display of wit, wisdom, confidence and intelligence.

Over the course of a few days and evenings we had the source of Themba Mashama's strength to feed on, a teacher who made the simplest movement a final exam question.

After the second lecture/demo was over we all understood how little we knew about Capoeira Angola and life. Mestre Moraes was Themba Mashama's stamp of certification. We were beginning to suspect that a different number was happening.

For example, the mestre's logic tripped some of us out for long moments.

"If you are right, then I am wrong. Are you right?"

A negativa was added to the ginga and a rastiera, and on the second day, a chapois de costa. It was like being a section of a classic construction of elements.

Questions and answers flew back and forth across the loft floor like bees swollen with nectar.

"Any questions?"

"Do you give out belts in Capoeira Angola?"

"What does the belt mean...? That you can twist somebody's head off? Could you twist somebody's head off if you didn't have a belt?"

"Batisados?"

"You have already been born; are you a better Angoliero because you have had a batisado?"

He stressed Africanity, constantly. "I am proud to be a Black man," linking it to the Religion.

"I have powers that I can call upon."

He added a role to the ginga-negativa-chapas and proved how powerful a weak person could become by moving in the right direction. He played complex games with our minds and stepped behind our struggling backs to announce, "I am here."

Or he circled us and playfully spanked our awkwardly moving butts. He trampled on the cosmetic manifestations of the ego without any mercy whatsoever.

"Why are you doing that?"

The stress, as always, mirroring the tradition that Mashama

honors, was on precision and excellence.

"If a mestre tells you to step here, step here! Do not step there or over there, step here! You understand?"

The tightly knit structure of Grupo de Capoeira Angola Pelourinho, an organization established by Mestre Moraes, Mestre Joao Grande and Mestre Cobrinha Mansa, was opened up to take Themba Mashama's Capoeira Angola Pequena under its wing.

Mestre Moraes added rabo de arraia on the fourth workshop day and continued stressing the need for civilized Pan-African behavior.

"We are people in different places. You are here, we are there. You understand?"

His humorous jabs at the various absurdities in modern life were so subtle that they often slipped past our heads before we caught the impact of the joke.

The humor depended on the unexpected twists and turns of a few words, the sudden switch from humor to non-humor, deadpan. Or with a sly smile and a musical laugh.

"Pay attention!" was a frequently heard command and there was no doubt that it meant—check out what I'm saying to you, be sensitive, push the wool out of your ears, listen like you've never listened before, be aware, pay attention!

He added a cold-blooded boca de calca to the ginga-negativa-rastiera-chapas-robe-rabo de arraia and talked candidly about the racial situation in Brazil, considered by some to be a racial paradise.

"We have serious problems with racism there also."

As a leader on the political-social scene in Bahia, he has been told that his life is in danger for espousing what we, the United States, once called Black Power.

"I am not afraid."

He extended his battleground by challenging us to support Capoeira Angola, as tangible evidence of our serious interest

82

in the promotion of the welfare of African people here and everywhere.

It was a "workshop" that didn't come to an end, in the conventional sense. We shared the feeling of having been taken to a higher, clearer level of thinking by a master teacher.

"Some day each of you may be called upon to teach Capoeira Angola. It is very important to understand that it is not muscles and strength, it is intelligence and movement."

We were left with as many thoughts and impressions as there were sisters and brothers who attended the sessions with Mestre Moraes. This is only one of them.

"Pay attention!"

Another Tango...

The Brother Who Had
Two Heads (for awhile)

There was always something a little different about my little brother Randolph.

I called him my "little" brother, despite the fact that I was only two years older, fourteen years old to his twelve, when this...uhhh...problem developed.

How was he different? Well, that would cover a lot of ground. Let me give you a few examples, okay?

Example: How many twelve-year-olds think about embalming as a career? That's right, don't switch channels!

The guy is talking about becoming an embalmer in a funeral parlor while the rest of his friends are thinking about becoming airplane pilots, doctors, basketball stars, movie actors, firemen, whatever.

"An *embalmer,* Randolph, why embalming?"

"Because embalmers get a chance to handle dead people. You know, something like the ending of a story."

See what I mean? It wasn't that the dude had both oars out of the water or anything like that. He was as smart as he could be. There was just that little bit of the Far Side to him, if you know what I mean.

Another example: He decided to invent his own personal language one day. He was ten years old at the time.

Why?! Who knows? All I can remember is that one day he was speaking "regulation" English and the next day he was walking around talking "Glibberdash."

That's what he called it: "Glibberdash."

I will never forget the sound of it as long as I live. Sorta like a cross between a crow cawing and an out of town salesman telling a bad joke.

After a few days of "Glibberdash" I was about to go out of my skull.

I made an appeal to Mom and Dad:

"Mom, Dad, could we do something about Randy?"

"What've you got in mind, Jerry?"

Mom was an artist and I can't ever remember talking to her when she wasn't sitting or standing in front of a canvas, or weaving, or doing Batik, or carving or something.

I proposed that we prohibit Randolph from speaking "Glibberdash," or any other similar sounding language.

My proposition actually caused Dad to lower his book (I never saw him at home without a book in his hands).

"But Jerry, don't you think that would be an abridgement of Randy's First Amendment rights?"

The matter was taken all the way up to a dinner table court session. There I was given the opportunity to present my argument.

I must say, even now, thirty-four years later, that my argument for the elimination of "Glibberdash" was eloquent, fanatical and completely subjective.

Randolph defended himself in "Glibberdash." Who really

knows what he said, but it was forceful enough to give us a tie vote. Mom was pro and Dad came up slightly con (with a bit of lobbying on my part).

Somehow the main issue was waylaid by parallel considerations ("If we do this, what's to prevent future assaults on freedom?"), which derailed the process so completely that we wound up with this tie.

I have reason to suspect that Mom and Dad may have indulged in a bit of chicanery on that one, but it didn't really matter.

A day later Randolph returned to the English-speaking world and that was the end of that.

"Randolph, what happened to 'Glibberdash?' "

"What do you mean, 'what happened?' "

"Well, Jerry, if you had paid as much attention to the language as you should have, rather than trying to have it outlawed, you would've discovered that the grammar was faulty. It was doomed to extinction."

Randolph could say stuff like that with a straight face, and mean every word.

But these are lightweight examples of how different my brother was. He really became a different character when he developed another head.

Let me explain...

We shared a bedroom and bunk beds, Randy on the bottom, me on the top. One morning (we were a month beyond "Glibberdash") Randy says to me from the bottom bunk, "Jerry, you can use the bathroom first."

I almost fell out of bed. I mean, we usually were close to hand-to-hand combat to determine who would get to brush his teeth first.

"Randy...you okay pal?" I asked him.

"Yeah, I'm okay, don't you want to use the bathroom first?"

I can still remember my puzzled face in the mirror. What was he up to?

I received a vague tipoff when I strolled back into our bedroom to find him fully dressed, complete with five yards of wool knit scarf around his neck.

Mom and Dad didn't seem to notice Randolph's odd addition to his summer shorts and Hawaiian sports shirt. If I remember correctly, Dad was re-reading *Being and Nothingness* and Mom was painting her fourth commissioned canvas.

In any event, they might not have noticed his scarf anyway, basically because he was not known to dress in any particular way. He read about the Spartans of ol' Greece and ran around in a T-shirt one winter; well, not the whole winter . . . people were constantly rushing up to him with shirts and coats.

He wore the scarf for days. It gave him a Quasimodo look.

"Randolph, the scarf, what's that about?"

"I like it."

I began to get very suspicious after he gave me privacy toilet privileges one whole week in a row. And it dawned on me that he was always dressed whenever he was in our room or anywhere.

"Randolph, what're you hiding?!"

"Nothing. Mind your own business."

I decided to spy on my brother. Yeah, it went against everything we'd been taught but I was totally curious.

We started our morning off as usual. Randolph giving me first rights to the bathroom. On this morning I pretended to go into the toilet but tipped back to peek through the door at Randolph.

Why was he being so secretive? Why was he dressing so quickly? What was the scarf all about?

I almost fainted peeking through the door.

My brother had something on the left side of his shoulder

87

that looked like another head.

I couldn't help myself. I stumbled back into the bedroom with my mouth wide open in surprise.

"Randolph, what the hell is that?"

He stared at me, obviously resigned to discussing my discovery. He perched on the edge of his bunk.

"I don't know, Jerry. I became aware of this thing about a month ago."

I was numb with fright and surprise. Here was my little brother sitting in front of me with a growth that looks like a duplication of his head, minus hair, eyes, lips and other features.

It wasn't a goiter—Dad had taught us all about goiters and stuff. No goiter here, this was a *head*.

"Are you in pain?"

He seemed quite nonchalant about the whole business, now that he had been exposed.

"Nope. It's more of an annoyance than anything else. And...it seems to be growing."

I fell down the last eight steps to get to Mom and Dad in the breakfast nook.

"Dad! Mom! Help! Come upstairs! Randolph is growing another head!"

Mom stared out of the window into the back yard for a pregnant moment and then jabbed Dad with an accusing glare.

"Godfrey, I told you we shouldn't have dropped that acid to conceive Randolph! Now look at what we've done!"

Dad, as calm as always, placed Zilowitz's *Study of Melanesian Schizophrenia* face down on the breakfast table.

"Yvonne, please. Don't become irrational. Let's go up and take a look at the...uhh...our son."

Randy hadn't moved. Mom fainted into the room. Dad,

88

the adventurer, slunk across the room and gave the growth a couple of light jabs with his right index finger.

"Randolph, looks like we're gonna have to buy you a different sized turtle neck sweater this winter."

In the weeks following we must've gone to a dozen hospitals; seen a dozen doctors. A half dozen more, having been alerted to this unusual happening, were called to ask if they could check Randolph's other head out.

The consensus was unanimous: It wasn't cancer, it wasn't a goiter, and it wasn't really another head. It just looked like one.

No one knew what to make of it, least of all Randy. He seemed half ashamed and half proud of the notoriety he was receiving:

Local Boy Grows Second Head.

"Hey, Jerry, you read this piece about me in the Sentinel?"

One day he was half ashamed, the next day he was proud.

"How many brothers have you had with two heads?"

I noticed that Dad took to reading a lot about mutations and Mom fell into what someone labeled her "Clone Period."

And just as suddenly as it arrived, it disappeared.

Like, one day it was there and the next day is was gone.

"Yeah, I noticed it this morning."

I could tell, from all of the unusual whispering that went on between Mom and Dad (they usually discussed everything openly—everything) that they were undecided about how they should react to the disappearance of Randolph's extra head.

They apparently reached a semi-neutral kind of position.

Dad: "Well, Randolph, I see that you've lost your head...I mean..."

Mom: "Ohhh, Randy, it's so good to see you one-headed again."

89

After awhile—post-dating Randy's graduation from high school with top grades for four years—we'd joke about the time he had two heads, for awhile.

"You know something, Jerry? The scariest part about that whole thing for me was whether or not I'd have to buy hats for both my heads for the rest of my life."

Randolph is still different, but he's matured quite a bit. He's not the type to lose his head over minor problems...if you know what I mean.

A Case of Mistaken Identity

I think I have to give my second grade teacher, Miss DuBois—we called her "ol' Hammerhead" behind her back—credit for becoming a writer, God rest her weary ol' bones.

Talk about being introduced to the creative world ass-backwards—that's just about the way it happened.

Ol' Hammerhead—or perhaps I should be more formal and call her Miss DuBois?—was one of the oldest, most decrepit, senile teachers in the school system.

She had taught my Aunt Bridget when she was in second grade. That's how long she'd been in the system. No wonder she'd speak in tongues all the time and get our names mixed up.

I guess, to be fair, you couldn't really blame her for being the way she was. Who knows how many years she had been traumatized or forced to remember how many thousands of names?

These weren't considerations I felt. Like back then, back when she was confusing me, Phil, with another guy in our class named Bill.

There was a slight similarity between us, aside from rhyming names, Phil/Bill: We were both light skinned, but the similarity stopped there.

Bill had thick, curly hair. Mine was of the more Africoid variety. He had a face full of freckles, I had none. He had a mouthful of rotten teeth. I didn't.

He was definitely a "bad seed," a really troublesome little asshole who might've been autistic (they weren't up on problem children in public schools back then. A few advances have been made), but I wasn't.

Miss Dubois couldn't make the distinction between us.

"Phil! she'd scream, when she really meant Bill. "Come up here to my desk!"

Her number was sadistic exhibitionism, or whatever the hell it's called when you love to whack people on the hands with a hard-edged, twelve-inch ruler in front of a room filled with bloodthirsty eight-year-olds.

"But Miss DuBois!"

"I saw you!" Whack! Whack! "Put your hand back up!" Whack! Whack!

She would, of course, catch Bill doing his share of dirt and whack him too, from time to time, but ninety percent of the time she whacked me, for Bill.

The lady's other frequently used torture weapon was an extended, right-hand foreknuckle. She often bored into the top of my head or into the temple area with this one.

Can you imagine the outrage you'd feel, simply sitting in class, humming a silly little tune while trying to figure out how many apples were left in the basket after John ate four out of ten, to suddenly find someone trying to bore a hole in your forehead with a jackhammer foreknuckle.

"Owwww! Miss DuBois! I didn't do nothin'!"

The lady had me on the edge of paranoia. I had to watch Bill closely, to make certain that I could get away with what he hadn't done. Which meant that there wasn't a helluva lot for me to do.

This was during the Golden Age of Scholastic Capital Punishment. No one even thought of going home to rat on the teacher (our parents believed that school was holy and teachers were sacred), or considered filing a class action lawsuit, or doing anything to correct the injustices that an innocent (relatively) eight-year-old might suffer at the hands of an "ol' Hammerhead."

We took the paddlings with the serrated ping pong paddles, we dodged the erasers flung at our head with Satchel Paige-like accuracy (ditto for the chalk missiles), stoically endured the hand whackings, accepted the uncomfortably appreciated fondlings of women teachers, stood in the corner with our dunce caps on our heads, and when we were failed (like I was), we blundered through the maze again.

"Phillip! Look at this report card! You've failed in every subject but recess. Wait 'til your father gets home!"

It was a blurred summer for me, the summer of my failure to pass into third grade. I spent days wandering around with my eyes glazed with tears that I couldn't shed; an ache in my body, somewhere between my heart and my stomach.

I thought about killing Bill so that we would never be mistaken for each other again. I thought about killing Miss DuBois so that she would never get me confused with anybody else. I thought evil thoughts about my unsympathetic parents.

"Boy, you keep this up and you might not graduate from grammar school 'til you're too old to vote."

I thought and I brooded a lot that summer. I gritted my

teeth a lot and started filling up loose leaf notebooks with stories about mice who could roar louder than lions, gnats who knew how to sting like bees, tiny people who could make giants howl with pain. .

Bill had passed, I hadn't. He was going on, I wasn't. My scribblings in my notebooks forced me to reconcile myself to the fact that I had failed but that I wasn't a failure.

But I was feeling somewhat evil by the time school started back in September; I had two notebooks of stories documenting my motivation.

Miss DuBois' look told me everything. I failed the wrong boy. This is Phil, not Bill. This is Phil, the good student who should be in third grade, not Bill...this is Phil, not Bill, Phil, not Bill, Phil, not Bill...

The repentant echoes in her eyes softened my malevolent attitude slightly, but not enough to prevent me from carrying out my vendetta. I had decided, over the summer, that I would become a "Bill."

My irrational reasoning gave me the reasons to act like an asshole. If I were going to be failed for being good Phil, what would happen if I became a bad Bill?

I acted out my worst behavioral fantasies that school year. I yanked front row braids.

"Miss DuBois! Phil pulled my hair!"

I chit-chatted during the so-called "quiet times." I created chaos during the course of any day and I was patiently endured. Childishly, I rubbed her semi-senile face in the mistake she had made.

When she asked the class to respond with a raised hand to the roll call, I would raise my hand and scream, "Bill!"

She never admitted that she had made a mistake, failing me and passing Bill, but when the semester ended I could see a light go out in her eyes.

During the course of my second week in the third grade

94

(taught by a Korean woman who thought African-Americans were savages) someone called out, "Hey! They takin' ol' Hammerhead out on a stretcher."

We rushed to the windows to see two attendants wheel a horse-blanketed figure out to an ambulance. We were close enough, on the first floor, to see and hear everything.

Miss DuBois looked okay, but it was obvious, from the crossbeamed look in her eyes, that all was not well.

She spotted me in the window and leaned up on her left elbow to wave and call out, "Good luck, Bill! Good luck!"

...The Cookie Crumbles...

What the hell, let's face it. Everybody gets a wild hair every now 'n then. When the sister approached me about making a drive to Chicago I didn't feel too enthused about the idea, at first. But after thinking on it a couple nights I started feeling like it was a good idea.

I was somewhat in between a couple of things at the time, so there was nothing to hold me back.

Before we go any further, let me make one thing absolutely clear: This wasn't a love thing of any kind. Me and Koko were friends from way back; had always been friends. You know how it is with some women, you just become friends and that's the way it stays.

I hadn't seen her in a couple years, but that's the way it happens in "El-A" sometimes. We'd talk on the phone from time to time, if we had any vital info to exchange. That kind of thing.

She had been a dancer at one point, heavily into that Ghanaian stuff. The deal now was for her to trip to Chicago for a gig in a club that one of her big-time ex-boyfriends had bought.

She had become a singer. I didn't know how good or how bad she was. It didn't matter to me one way or another.

She wanted me to make the drive with her because she'd never driven beyond Long Beach and has glaucoma, which means she couldn't drive at night.

"You haven't seen me in awhile. I've gained twenty pounds. Maybe we could work out and fast as we go. What do you think?"

"Sounds like a good idea to me. When do we leave?"

"How 'bout June 26th?"

She calls on June 24th.

"Looks like we're going to have to postpone for a couple days."

"No big thing. Oh, incidentally, Koko, I wanted to talk with you about the return trip. How long are you planning to stay?"

"About two weeks. That cool with you?"

"That sounds just right. I'll have enough of Chicago by then I'm sure."

"If I should decide to stay longer, I'll pay for your airfare back."

"That's a deal."

Hmmmm . . . the sister must've won a piece of the lottery. June 26th.

"Look, uhhh, this check hasn't come yet, why don't we think about leaving on the 28th?"

"The 28th? That sounds okay. Hope nothing else comes up. I'm beginning to get a little antsy, you know what I mean?"

"I heard that."

97

By this time I had repacked my bags to downright perfection; I was ready to go.

June 28th.

"Uhhh, this is Koko. We won't be able to get on the road today, something came up. But we can definitely leave on the 30th."

I was semi-pissed.

"Koko, are you really sure you want to make this trip?"

"Oh yes, definitely! I'll be over to pick you up at 11:00 a.m., day after tomorrow."

"See you when you get here." I seriously thought about cancelling out.

June 30th. She picks me up on time.

"Is that all the stuff you're bringing?"

"This is it, a little bag and a big bag."

"Good."

Her car is loaded from the trunk to the front seat: saltine crackers, trunks of stuff, cold drinks in a freezer, a sound system.

"They might not have what I need in this place."

The professional is always prepared. Okay, sounds sensible to me.

We must, she says, return to her place for a few more things (what the hell else can we put in the car?) and a last minute shower. No problem.

I thought it might be wise to make an ebo before we get on the road. Everything helps.

While she's in the shower I trip to get the ingredients for the offering. It's a brutally hot day in "El-A"; a perfect day to move.

I waited impatiently for her to finish the longest shower anybody ever took.

My head is lolled back in a Patience Mode. Damn! Women are slow as peanut butter.

She strolled past me, from the bathroom to the kitchen, stark raving naked. I remember thinking, maybe she forgot I was here. Or maybe she doesn't give a damn. Who cares? Let's go!

But I was really puzzled. After all, it was a helluva display. Oh well...

We finally got down to the overloaded car. She had to run back up to do something three times before we could finally pull off. Woww, I'm thinking, how indecisive can you be?

We're traveling on her plastic, will rent motel rooms for us if we become too tired. We're friends from way back. Her ex ol' man doesn't feel threatened by our trip. Everything is on track. Maybe.

Hot as hell, but we got AC, which we'll use sparingly to save the car.

The drive is on and she's talking. She has been talking for the whole time, come to think of it. I noticed that some of the stuff was disassociated, but I pinned that down to prime time excitement.

She talked and talked and talked. I was beginning to think there might be some weird spin off benefits to this. I'll have a chance to think while she asks and answers her own questions.

Hot as hell.

We're exhausted. Or rather I should say, I was exhausted from driving straight out from "El-A" to Ashfork, Arizona. We popped into town at 2:00 a.m. on a Saturday night and couldn't find a vacant room anywhere because the rodeo was in town.

An Indian (East, not West) motel clerk named Dromesh found room in his personal inn for us.

"I can rent you the room I sleep in—this one behind the desk here—but there is no double bed however."

He was puzzled by us signing our names separately.

"Are you not together?" he asked.

"Yes, we are also apart," I answered.

Koko simply rolled her eyes and quick-stepped into the room.

One large bed, one small room. I shuffled to the shower, cleaned myself up, put on my karate pants and dived into my side of the bed. An hour later I was still trying to go to sleep.

The lady had bucked into a black negligee and was practicing faces in the mirror on the dresser and talking to me.

"I know you want me to get in bed with you, so you can rape me, but that's not going to happen."

I sat up in bed, trying to convince her that I was too tired to want anybody. And besides, she was my friend, not a potential mate of any kind.

I finally forced myself to sleep, nodding off with the realization that I was traveling with someone who had a real problem. A nervous breakdown, at least. It jarred me to sleep.

Next morning. Where is she? You couldn't stay up all night, making faces in the mirror, and talking all night, and get up early.

I decided to watch closely for pill popping.

She was in the cafeteria attached to the motel, one of those tacky places where the food is oily, plentiful and deadly.

I checked her out at the eating bar, dressed theatrically: the Gone-with-the-Wind hat, dark glasses, bullfight blue jeans opened three buttons from the top, all the better for her to add five more pounds of biscuits (heavily buttered and jellied), bacon, grits, toast (good with biscuits), milk, eggs, other stuff coming.

I came close to running off to the nearest bus station.

It didn't seem fair to do it like that, I had made a

commitment to help drive to Chicago. I felt that I had to honor that commitment. We were "married," for three days at least, for better or worse.

"Koko, why are you stomping on the brakes, baby?"

Black people are always overt to nuances in words, the tone has to be right. I prayed that mine was.

"Didn't you see that truck brake to a stop?"

"No, Koko, the truck slowed down to turn a curve. He didn't stop. And besides, he's at least a half mile ahead of us. Why put on your brakes this far away?"

I became slightly unglued. What the fuck have I let myself in for?

"Koko, you shouldn't drive on the white line like that, you're in the center of the highway."

"Didn't you read that sign back there that said—'Stay on the median?'"

"It said stay *off* the median. Off! Off!"

"What's the median got to do with driving down the center of the highway?"

I felt sick to my stomach. Truck drivers brushed past us, playing terrified chicken.

I didn't know whether to slug her and try to wrestle the wheel from her or just jump out of the car. I compromised with myself and went to sleep.

I was formulating a plan; I took a fatalistic sleep. I had to rest myself so that I could drive all night and half the next day. I calculated that that would put us in Illinois.

I slept the sleep of the fatalist. I was praying that I wouldn't be killed in my sleep, and that I would be allowed to get behind the wheel just one more time.

Night falling on us in Texas (or was it New Mexico?) saved my life. Even she had to admit that she wasn't driving well.

"I can't see shit!"

She finally surrendered the wheel after a near collision with

101

a signpost on the right side of the highway.

"Here, why don't you drive for awhile?"

What I though was Texas was really New Mexico. Tears cropped up in my eyes. Damn!

We stopped for gas and she loaded up on Twinkies, cigarettes, barbecued pig's feet, potato chips, Snickers candy bars. The nausea that gripped my belly almost caused me to puke.

But I was determined to stick it out.

It jumped outright hostile between us on Sunday afternoon. We stopped to do exercises at a rest stop (on of the weight controlling measures she had asked for) and she went into the ladies' room to change and came out with this halter and these cut-up-the-side running shorts that allow three fourths of her gushy tail to fall out.

What to do? How does one say, "Check yourself out, sister. You look like the lowest class 'ho ever seen at a rest stop."

The good ol' boys resting their rigs nutted out at the sight of this unexpected striptease. I felt like a betrayed ally.

"Look, Koko, don't you have anything else? You know, something a bit less revealing? How about leotards?"

"Don't try to tell me what to wear!" she snapped back, and started a slow forward stretch that exposed the hairs of her stuff.

I withdrew from her sphere and started doing situps on a picnic table. There was nothing else to do.

Back on the road (it's daytime, she insists on driving), she started rantin' 'n ravin' about Black men and white women. The usual.

Peripherally, I watched her swallow a couple mystery pills, rant and rave, drive. I honestly got scared, for the first time. Is she on a suicide trip? Where do I fit into all this?

"Mandela is a hero to everybody but you, why is that?"

102

"So why shouldn't I wear shorts? White women wear 'em. You like to see white women in shorts, don't you?!"

I'm getting pissed; losing control of myself.

"I like to see women in shorts who have asses that fit inside, not those that gush all out 'n shit!"

Even if she's having a nervous breakdown I can't see any reason for taking crap.

"You goddamned motherfucker you!"

I'm driving now. It's dark. I stopped the car and threatened to break her fuckin' jaw if she called me out of my name again. She must've realized how serious my threat was and immediately redialed her number.

"I didn't call you out of your name. I was just cursing in general."

I was beginning to feel sorry for her. I mean, after all, I knew her from way back, before she stepped off the edge.

But there was no time for a lot of pity. I refocused on my objective—get where you're going so you can get away from all this madness.

I drove from Sunday evening (or was it Monday? Did I hallucinate?) to Monday morning, half listening to a conversation she was having with a variety of people.

From time to time she slipped back into a "normal" mode and we concentrated on ways to deal with her problem.

"Why don't you see a psychologist when we get back to L.A., Koko?"

"I may not go back."

"Well, why don't you see one wherever you are?"

She sneered and started back into the pile of junk food in her lap.

It's night. I'm driving again. She has finally fallen asleep for a few minutes. We're in Illinois, the light is blinking to me from the end of the tunnel.

"Take me back!"

Back? What the hell is she talking about now?

"Back where?"

"To California; to L.A."

We pulled into a rest stop (Pontiac, Illinois, 100 miles south of Chi—hooray!). She's trying to call her sister who lives somewhere in that area.

She's crying, she's unhappy. She wants to drive.

"But it's night, Koko. You can't see at night, remember?"

She jumps back in the car after three unsuccessful attempts to call her sister, locks the doors and sits there spilling out these huge teardrops. Never saw tears that large before.

A survival nerve cued me to take my large bag out of the trunk immediately (she had given me a duplicate set of keys at the beginning), but my totebag with all of my ID was in the back seat.

"Koko, lower the window and give me by totebag. Please."

I felt tempted to take a large rock and shatter the side window, pull a commando raid for my stuff. The headlines in the Pontiac Register throbbed through the back of my mind.

"Niggershit at the rest stop. Details on page ten."

I called the police and prayed that she couldn't drive away before they got there. *I* called the police.

Officer Vedder hopped out of the car lickety split; poked me in the belly with his club.

The little voice of African-in-America survival tactic #101 whispered, "be cool."

I ignored his racist animosity and explained in dry, neutral, straight ahead white folks' legalese what the fuckin' problem was.

"Not only am I trying to get my totebag with all of my ID out of the back seat, I'm trying to save her life by

104

preventing her from driving in the dark. She has glaucoma.''

He still wanted to beat me up, just to say he had whipped a coon last night, but he decided to put me on the back burner for a sec.

"Roll your winder down, Miss."

She rolls her window down sweetly, shows her glaucoma medicine to him and a license with no driving restrictions.

I felt like a Twilight Zone person. How can you have a serious case of glaucoma and a license with no restrictions?

The crackercop takes her license, checks his computer for larceny, can't figure out the angle he wants to start whippin' my head from, asked a few more questions.

"Why did you put in a call?"

She blinks eyelashes at him from the driver's seat.

"Officer, he tried to attack me."

I could feel the stick begin to slip up from the holder on his belt. I countered as fast as my nerves would allow.

"Officer, I called in, remember? It's recorded on the police station tape."

The Neanderthal brow knitted for a full five minutes. He was obviously trying to figure out a way to whip my ass, rape Koko, and shoot the car in three quick movements.

"Give this boy his stuff from outta there!"

She dimpled audaciously and obeyed immediately. I had my stuff, I was in Illinois, I was saved.

He gave both of us a hard look before driving off. She followed him into the darkness beyond the rest stop, bellowing curses out at me.

"You dirty rotten sonovabitch! You vicious dog motherfucker! You asshole cocksuckin' son of a bitch! Gawddamn you! You! You...!''

I almost sank to my knees to give thanks to the Ancestors. I felt as though my life had been spared and that I had been redeemed.

Now then, how does one get a ride into Chicago at 2:30 a.m.?

My problem was solved at dawn by a Carol Burnett-looking farm hand who decided to let her guard down, this once.

"You're not an escaped convict or anything, are you?"

She refused the twenty dollars I offered, but she studied my driver's license and passport for ten minutes.

I felt like a Roman emperor riding into Chicago in the back of her pickup.

"I don't know you so I can't let you ride in the cab with me."

Any deal was a good deal after Koko.

"No problem."

Cold trip in the back of the pickup. Cold.

She dropped me off with a timid handshake, five miles from my destination.

"Thank you."

"You're welcome."

My friends were gathered on the terrace of their beautiful home near the lake when the taxi driver helped me out of his taxi.

"Well now, what have we here?"

I had to smile, it was just the kind of question Fred would ask.

Lynn, more pragmatic in her way: "How was the trip?"

I was still sobbing over my third glass of White Horse before I realized I couldn't explain what the trip did to me. I may never be able to explain.

I wonder how Koko would describe it.

106

The Key

Vincent turned the key in the lock and slowly opened the door, the way he always did when he came into the apartment.

He closed the door and strolled through the apartment, a one-bedroom, furnished affair in the semi-bohemian University area. The "main room," a tiny kitchen with a pygmy refrigerator, a rolled out sofa bed with two futons covering the mattress, a view of the lakefront from the east side window, the stereo and bookcase on the opposite wall.

He stared at the half-empty bottle of Beaujolais on the low table in the center of the main room.

Tania loved red wines, especially the Beaujolais.

"You know that toast the Spanish make? May there be more of this blood for your blood."

He pulled the cork from the bottle and tilted it up to his mouth for a long sip. The wine was thick, warm, fragrant.

...Still a half bottle of wine left and I'm back, waiting for another woman already.

A tight smile crinkled the corners of his mouth.

Another woman already...

He stood in front of the east-side window, sipping wine and staring down onto the scenes he had grown to love, sharing this apartment that Tania had named "Our Love Spot."

The meticulously manicured garden of the old Italian couple next door, the crazy profusion of fruit trees in the yard next to it, the wide slash of grass a few blocks away on the lakefront.

He could see the place where they had sprawled one warm spring afternoon and made a deal.

"Vince, why does it have to be 'your place' or 'my place?' Why not 'our place?' "

Vincent shared an apartment with two other men; Tania shared a rented house with three other women.

The "Love Spot" was their place—had been their place.

"I mean, let's face it—we're lovers without a spot to love in. I don't feel quite right going to your place. I know, I'm old fashioned in some ways. And you're not comfortable with Mary, Helen and Joyce around..."

The "Love Spot" was passed onto them by a mutual friend, a graduate student who was off on a six-month archeological dig in the Middle East.

"Johnny's giving us his place for four months. All we have to do is pay the utilities. What do you think, Vince?"

The first shared, thin-crusted pizza sealed their commitment.

"Tania, you know something?"

"What?"

"I'm glad you let me talk myself into this."

They spent their days doing what was necessary (Vincent

Franklin, the successfully working thirty-year-old stockbroker; Tania Beltran, the twenty-five-year-old computer analyst), desperately waiting for evenings and weekends.

One of Tania's roommates had labeled them "the lust demons."

"Tania, this is Vince..."

"I'll be the first car out of the parking lot, why don't you pick up a bottle of Beaujolais Villages?"

The passion they shared quickly moved them up to the kinds of naked discussions they relished. And hated.

"I've never felt like this before with a man."

"How many men have you been with?"

"Not a whole bunch. Am I the first woman you've ever made love to?"

Sprawled out side by side on the doubled futons gave them another world, another dimension to explore.

"Tania, you ever come here by yourself?"

"I've never even thought about it."

He strolled away from the window, delicately sipping the wine. Twenty-five disks in the record storage rack: Spanish flamenco (to commemorate Tania's six months stay in Spain), Indian ragas by Alla Akbar Khan and Ravi Shankar, lots of avant garde jazz, Afro-Cuban percussion, a few ol' fashioned symphonies and concertos.

He checked his watch. Clotilde is so punctual. What the hell made me come here an hour early?

Clotilde Hood was the opposite of Tania Beltran in every way he could think of. Clotilde was tall and slim—Tania, short and voluptuous. Tania was impulsive, warm—Clotilde, somewhat calculating and aloof, almost snobbish.

He sat on the edge of the futon-covered sofa. How many times had they raced to the apartment, for two months, panting to make love...? And, as suddenly as they were drawn into their passion, they were thrown out of it. It started with an argument.

"Really, Vincent! I can't see why you can't keep the place clean! I certainly do my share!"

Who was to blame for the escalation of hostility?

"Tania, I thought we were going to be together on Saturday."

"Vince, don't you think you're taking our relationship a little bit for granted?"

Who was to blame? She is, Vince answered his own question.

Two broken dates sealed their fate.

"Vince, I thought we were going to be together Friday. I was there and you weren't. You know, it occurred to me for the first time that you're the one with the key."

"You want a duplicate?"

"What do I need with a key if you're going to be there?"

"Tania—what happened, baby? What're you trying to do, make me distrust you?"

He sprawled back on the bed. What can I do to let her know that I love her? He sat up slowly, took another sip of wine.

I *do* love her. I do love her. What was the problem anyway? A few angry words. How many people have lost someone they truly cared for because they had made vicious statements while they were angry about something?

The flavor of all the beautiful hours they had spent together, in this apartment, suddenly welled up inside of him.

Maybe it's the wine. The wine and the memory of these hours caused him to leave the sofa bed and pace around the apartment.

We haven't seen each other for two weeks and I'm already making dates with other women. Men are such dogs. I'll bet she's ten feet from the phone, praying that I'll call.

Once again he paused in front of the window. Why don't I call?

The idea jarred him for a second. Why don't I call her? What about Clotilde? He bit on his bottom lip, thinking.

Awww, what the hell! What was it going to be anyway? A little fun? A few games? A little sex? Lots of laughs?

He drained the last sip of wine from the bottle and returned the empty to the table. Hope she's at home. I'd be mad as hell if I call and she isn't there.

He paused in the open door. Wonder what Clotilde will think when she gets here and I'm not here. Maybe I should leave her a note.

Nawww, that wouldn't do. What if Tania found it. I'll just call her up and be honest about the whole thing.

The smug smile was sliced from his face by the sight of Tania climbing up the steps of the apartment building, followed by a tall, slender, dark-skinned man with a lascivious gleam in his eyes.

Other Tangos . . .

My Favorite Things
(The Park)

There are three ways to get into the Park, one is to drive up this gently sloped road, another is to dive out of a helicopter and land in the front of the Gallery.

The most interesting way is to walk up the steps facing Hollywood Boulevard at New Hampshire. The people assembled at the second landing of the steps make it interesting. A mulled crew hangs out there: a few mystics who stare up at the Observatory for days on end, brutal looking white and Black men, Mexicans, Filipinos, a stray Indian, winos, dopers, losers, professional burglars (they talk openly in front of familiar strangers), people waiting on a job to open up, or for a rock to give way to a hard place, at least. A wasted lady (they talk openly in front of familiar strangers), people off the street.

The second landing tenants are ingenious and many of them have discovered a way to live in the park for weeks,

112

undisturbed, and not disturbing. They simply live there. On a recent visit, it was noted that an electric skillet had been plugged into the park's power system; the skillet held an elegant arrangement of chicken breasts and fresh bell pepper rings.

From time to time, hostilities threaten to surface and it may seem dangerous to pass through their midst, but they only appear to want to do harm to themselves, the "In" crowd. Past the steps, 'round the curve, we get into the places in the park.

The pottery, painting, Ikebana building on the right and up the slope to the main stem. Barnsdall, from the front (north side), opens the eyes as you ascend the steps. The Gallery facade, the great pines, eucalyptus and poplar, the sensibly designed walks, make the place a pleasure to see.

The mountains out there and the Italian Riviera homes climbing up the sides of Silverlake, Echo Park, the slightly cleaner air draws people.

Harry strolls through the park, lost in artistic thought, cigarette at port arms, coffing! coffing! a troika of Snauzers strung out in front of him.

"'Mornin' Marvin."

"Hi Harry."

A brief, punchy conversation about everything, Harry reads. "Mrs. Lebanon," eyes kohl ringed and bright, pauses to join the conversation, on the guard for strays who might try to mount her "Taksim."

The Newspaper Reader, thin as a string, eyes glazed from the *Herald Examiner* and the *Times*, leaves his seat at the picnic table, filled with updated tragedies, drops the newspapers into the nearby trash can and shuffles away, a ghost until tomorrow.

Bob retrieves the paper, under the clicking shudders of a bunch of HollyHock House tourists. Frank Lloyd Wright

113

would've dug Bob's action, no doubt, making use of what the environment had to say.

The sun begins to dapple through the olive trees, pulling a sextet of old Armenian men, berets cocked, "worry beads" behind them, to the picnic table for a haunted game of cards.

A Black woman, obviously middle aged and pregnant, twists her left heel behind her head, untwists, and then does the same with her right foot. A fascinated bunch of six-, seven- and eight-year-olds, taking a fountain break from the Junior Arts Center, stare at the yoga woman. The yoga woman tilts her head to the sun and massages her breasts and belly.

High noon now and a young man, not racially definable, the sun has turned his features into a Cordovan brown, moves through the park as though he were being jerked along by heavenly strings. He giggles into the atmosphere and points at sliding images.

The men who empty the trash cans, water the park in the dry season, clean up the dog shit and trim everything trimmable, turn discreet eyes on all of this.

They've seen all kinds of sex acts on the southeast slope, the dope and liquor parties, and remain cool.

"Hey, lookit! If that's what they like to do, it's fine with me. It ain't nothin' but a different kind of way of lovin'."

On some days, when there is honey on the air and a John Coltrane mood filters through the trees, from somewhere on the left, children pause in their play, cock their heads as though listening to sounds too high for adults to hear.

The place becomes almost a contradiction, at times, but that doesn't really matter. What's important to remember is that there are three ways to get into the park and no way to get out, not if you feel it for what it is.

Perdido

AlGoBu R. the First shuffled to a seat by the window, leaning heavily on his shepherd's staff. It had been a long, long journey.

He settled himself as comfortably as possible, ignoring the curious looks people gave his multicolored caftan, his goatskin diddy bag, his gnarled, six-foot staff and the raccoon-eyed mask that topped his Old Testament beard.

Yes, it had been a long, long journey, he sighed quietly, and this was the last leg of it.

He pulled a small piece of sheepskin parchment from a hidden pocket of his robe...1313 East Jerusalem Street...stared at it as he had done many times before and carefully replaced it. The Sacred Address...Salvation.

Riding underground disturbed him, the dank feeling of the dark tunnel and the noise of the train clattering against his ears, but it was an easier ride than being on a camel's back, or trying to handle a sealskin kayak.

The train suddenly burst from the dark tunnel and began to slowly raise itself to the second-story level of the building bordering the tracks.

AlGoBu stared, hypnotized by the sight of the city flickering past his eyes. A great soup of people made it all the more interesting...the blacks, whites, browns and yellows, and here and there, a subtle shade in between.

He swiveled a bit in his seat to glance at the people riding to the east with him, a reflection of what he was seeing on the streets below.

He could sense, deep within his soul, that it would only be a matter of time before he reached his Destination, the goal of a journey of many years. Silently he chanted, "wooo blah dee oohh papa daa, wooo blah dee ooohhh papa daaa," and made the Sacred Sign of the Circle.

A stranger in a strange land, he felt, after these many years, a sudden twinge of homesickness, a quick rush of fear at the possibility that he might be on the wrong train going in the wrong direction.

Remembering his trans-Siberian train mistake of years before, he turned to the lady who had occupied the seat next to him, wrinkling her nostrils at the heroic fragrances of frankincense, stale hay, myrrh and camel's piss.

"East?" he mouthed the word, afraid to attempt to deal with any other words in this difficult language.

The lady, a small, dark-skinned, heavyset, middle-aged sister, nibbling surreptitiously from a family dinner box of Colonel Sanders' chicken, her day of domestic service over, stared at his mouth and then his mask.

"Huh?" she said, wrinkling an already wrinkled brow even more.

"East?" he asked again, pantomiming his question this time. She looked closely at his mask and the urgent gesture

116

he made. Oh well, what the hell, lotsa people are havin' it tough these days.

Without a change of expression, she wrapped a chicken thigh in a paper napkin and handed it to him.

"I can't give you none o' my soda 'cause I ain't opened it yet," she spoke to him in a joking tone...and hurriedly gathered her shopping bag and chicken box for a quick exit, "Ooppps, 39th Street, my stop!"

AlGoBu R. the First stared at the crisply browned chicken thigh, waved to the lady hurrying to validate her transfer, and back to the chicken.

The signs were right, this act of kindness was an indication, he was definitely headed in the right direction. No sweat. He flashed a smile full of stained teeth at the lady's memory and gnawed the chicken down to the bone's marrow.

A quick glance around after his dinner puzzled his mind for a few seconds...all of the people on the train had become black, whereas, a few stops ago, there had been more of a mixture. What difference does it make? he shrugged the question away and made the Sign of the Circle to validate his U.S.-ness.

"How 'bout it, mister man? You wanna buy a *Jet*?"

AlGoBu redirected his attention to the owner of the raspy voice, a muscular, ten-year-old version of a man trying to earn an honest American buck.

AlGoBu nodded gently, no, no thank you, and instinctively chanted a quiet blessing onto the hard-working youngster's being, "wooo blah dee ooohh papa daaa, wooo blah dee oohh papa daaa, wooo blah dee oohhh papa daaa."

The juvenile entrepreneur screwed his full mouth up with scorn and moved on, muttering, "Jive ass turkey...*Jet! Jet* for you, Miss Lady? How 'bout you, brother, got a nice centerfold this week."

AlGoBu turned benign eyes onto the swarming streets of

117

the deep summertime Southside. Forty-third Street.

The seat next to him became the owner of a man who seemed, at first glance, to be a woman, but a harder look disclosed a very clean-shaven, rouged, sweet-smelling, black transsexual, of the Sir Lady Java genre.

"Couple papers for you brothers?"

The superneat, Black Muslim newspaper vendor bowed at the edge of their seat with two copies of *Muhammad Speaks* already folded. AlGoBu looked puzzled as his seat mate dug down into a crocheted change purse for payment for two papers.

"Here, honey," he/she placed both newspapers on AlGoBu's lap and gave his left thigh a heavy pinch while doing so. "I buy this damned paper," he/she whispered, "every time one o' them Muslams comes up to me but I ain't read one yet. Is you a Muslam, honey?"

Before AlGoBu had a chance to formulate an answer, six members of the Golden Rods, upon whose turf the train was "trespassing," mounted the train. Forty-seventh Street.

"Ohh, my goodness! here comes Trouble, Bad Vibes, Evil, Sin, Dirty Words and Foul Behavior," he/she eased away to another car, giving his thigh a final loving pinch.

The young gangsters swept through the car, doing a simple, complete job of terrifying everyone, except AlGoBu.

He had seen and had experiences with the very same types in Afghanistan and Tibet, and knew exactly what to do if they showed any sign of doing anyone any real harm.

AlGoBu measured the move he'd have to make in order to win the fight.

He gripped his staff a little firmer in his calloused hand.

"Heyyy mannnn, you got any spare change?" one of the gangsters, a snaggle-toothed fifteen-year-old asked him, a small, nasty looking butcher knife backing up the question.

"Awww, c'mon, brotherman, let that nut alone! Can't you

118

see? He a bandit, just like us!'' the leader called out to his follower. The fifteen-year-old reluctantly gave up the idea of robbing AlGoBu and disembarked with his companions. Fifty-first Street.

The people in the car breathed a little easier, the danger past, the carnivorous animals having moved on to other prey. AlGoBu moved his lips in a grateful chant to the U.S. for having saved them from being hurt by a less sensitive group of human beings.

''Wooo blah dee ooohh papa daaa, wooo blahhh dee oohh papa daaa, woooo blah dee ohh papa daaaa.''

A clean-cut, *Essence* magazine-type couple seated across from him stared curiously as they caught his index finger making the Sacred Sign of the Circle in the center of his forehead. Fifty-fifth Street...a congenital drunk.

He flopped his head to an oblique angle for a few minutes, studying AlGoBu from top to bottom.

''Sayyyyy, mannnnn, you got a...uhhh...you got a cig...a cig...a cigareet?''

AlGoBu nodded no, patiently, remembering his own days and ways with the succulent grape in years past. And the mornings after. The drunk lurched against him as the train pulled away to the next stop.

''You got a mask on,'' the sloshed dude stated flatly.

AlGoBu nodded in agreement and braced the man in his seat to prevent him from slipping down onto the floor.

''What's the mask for?'' he asked finally, slurring each word, after AlGoBu had firmly braced him in place.

AlGoBu R. the First, puzzled as to which words he should make an attempt to use, to try to explain the why of the mask, received unexpected help from the couple across the aisle.

''C'mon, ol' timer, here's your stop *and* a pack o' cigarettes,'' the clean-cut, young *Essence* mag dude said, and diplomatically eased the drunk off the train at 61st Street.

"Don't pay him no mind," the *Essence* man said casually, as he returned to his lady, "he always buggin' people, from 55th to 61st, that's his route."

AlGoBu traded shy smiles with the *Essence* dude's lady and breathed a sigh of relief...wooo blah deee ooohhh papa daa, wooo blah deee ohhh papa daaa...and Circled them.

They were fascinated by his movements, but maintained their quintessentially *Essence* cools.

AlGoBu felt tempted to pull his Destination Address out of his robe and ask them if they knew where it was, but decided not to, like, after all, the young man had troubled himself enough already to rid him of a petty nuisance.

He looked back down onto the passing scene with renewed interest as the train wound around the curve at 63rd Street. This Southside was black, but unlike any Africa he had ever known.

The music bubbling from the windows lining the train tracks was difficult to understand, but easy to listen to.

That, and the lifestyle of a people who seemed to be moving and standing still at the same time. All of it done in time to some rhythm that he could not quite make out.

At every intuitive point that he felt he was coming close to grasping a certain feeling, a sensibility, a certain Nuance, another movement was made, denying the validity of the understanding he felt he had had only moments ago.

The couple across from him smiled sympathetically at the frown on his face.

"Seat taken?" the tall, young white man with a full auburn beard asked him, gesturing with the Bible to the space next to AlGoBu.

Before he could answer, "No, not taken," the young man sank into the seat and asked, a super-serious expression on his face, "My friend, do you know Jesus?"

AlGoBu blinked, surprised at the idea that a total stranger

would question his relationship with a relative.

A slight, cautious nod was all that was needed to launch the young man off onto an inspired spiel.

"Jesus, you see, is everywhere. I say unto you, as it is written, so shall it be."

AlGoBu lapsed from surprise to embarrassment for the young man's behavior, for his odd way of asking and answering his own questions.

"Is Jesus the answer? yes! emphatically yes! Jesus is, without question, the answer!" "He that believeth in Me shall have everlasting life!" "Yea, though I walk through the shadows of the Valley of Death, I fear no evil, for the Lord is with me." The *Essence* couple alternately frowned and smiled at AlGoBu's predicament.

The Jesus freak bounced from his seat as the train slid into his stop.

"Remember, friend...you've got to have Jesus in your life at all times, both night and day!"

AlGoBu nodded compassionately and made the Sign of the Circle at the Jesus freak. The freak stared at AlGoBu's face from the station platform as the train pulled away.

"Wait! Hold it! I want to," he called out, chasing the moving train, "wait! I want to talk to..."

"Wooo blah dee ooohh papa daaa, wooo blah dee, oohhh papa daaa, wooo blah dee oohhh papa daaa," AlGoBu chanted softly.

The "B" trained moved on, pulled into its final stop at 63rd and Stony Island.

AlGoBu R. the First, refreshed by the encounters and situations he had just felt and been a part of, made his way uncertainly down the station steps to the street.

"1313 East Jerusalem?" he asked the first person he met at the street level.

The old man, in a high-crowned, unblocked black hat, with

121

Shirley Temple curls for sideburns, stared at AlGoBu for a few hard seconds.

"If you walk three hundred blocks that way," he answered, pointing west, "You won't come to it, but...if you keep walking that way," pointing eastward, "you might find the address and your beard floating at the same time."

"Thank you," AlGoBu said solemnly and leaned heavily on his staff as he made his way to the lakefront.

"Who was that masked man?" the *Essence* couple asked the man that AlGoBu had spoken to.

The old man stroked his beard a few times as they watched AlGoBu walk, his sandals not touching the ground.

"I dunno, I got my suspicions," he answered and made the Sign of the Circle as he started after AlGoBu with a fast shuffle, mumbling into his beard, "wooooooo blahhh deee, oooohhh papa daaaa, wooooo blahhhh dee ooohhh papa daaa, wooo blahhh deee ooohhh papaaa..."

Kanoon's Concerto

Kanoon Al-Haddi, once known, before his conversion to Islam, as Milfred Hawkins, stood center stage playing an African thumb piano. Bathed in a luminous blue spotlight, his precious bassoon perched on a stand beside him.

The Pot's Monday night jazz audience, a confection of semi-professional musicians, professional musicians, hip-deep believers, cool dudes and their ladies sat mesmerized by Kanoon's passionate involvement with his art.

During the course of the playing of one particularly tricky phrase, Kanoon looked out at the audience, tears forming in his eyes, lips trembling, and moaned.

"Git down, Kanoon! Git on down to stone soul!" a high Gemini lady, unable to bear her erotic tension, called out to him.

Flicking into and through the phrase again, satisfied that he was getting exactly what he wanted, he slid away from it and signaled, with an arrogant turn of his head, for the re-entrance of his quintet.

The quintet's sound, Mediterranean-Afro-Cuban-Blues-New World, danced past his staccato thumbing, the little box held up close to the microphone wobbled back artfully to the last phrase he had played and slithered to an end.

The audience stood as one and applauded wildly.

Kanoon bowed ever so slightly, a cold smile flickering from his full beard.

Good, really good, he thought, to see the people giving themselves up to Another Music.

He nodded solemnly to the members of his group, sharing the applause with them, taking the measure of each one as he did so.

Sheikh Baby on the oud. Buford Knobbs doing it on every sized flute currently known, doubling on chekere and double gong. Pablo Cruz-Extrana playing the cello with so much quickness and grace that people were always asking why the dude was playing this oversized guitar, standing on end like that.

Them, that is, who weren't hip to the fact that Cruz-Extrana was a genius.

Baby Blood blew soprano sax and loved ragaic solos, always gave the impression of being angry at somebody, or something, but showed none of that kind of feeling as he spooled out note after note of brutally beautiful song.

"Concerto for Bassoon!" someone else picked up the refrain.

He stood at the edge of the stage and let them come at him in full voice before he reached for his instrument.

"Yeahhh! Gon' put the pot on!"

"Cook!"

"Concerto for Bassoooon, Kanooooon!"

"Right on!"

124

He picked his bassoon up from its stand, glared the audience into submissive silence, paused to deep breathe a full minute, to tune in with the members of his group, and gestured the music into being..."Uh one, uh two, uh one two three!"

Cruz-Extrana loved the Concerto and it showed in his method of approach.

A so-called jazz critic, unable to get past Pablo's long black eyelashes and his slender, delicately tapered fingers, called his opening statement the Chinese Blues.

Pablo and Kanoon laughed themselves to tears reading the review. It was obvious that the reviewer had never heard of saeeta nor had he ever heard La Nina de los Peines or Manitas de Plata's cousin, Jose Reyes, sing one...which logically denied him any recognition of Pablo's cello saeeta. Kanoon slipped Baby Blood in behind the cello's opening statement, nodding warmly at the Baby's deep, searching, artfully slurred sounds.

Buford swiped at the Baby's rail ends with little melodic swoops and whoops, Sheikh Baby counterpointed with his oud, Armandito calmly put the chekere aside and got down on his congas with a rhythmic pattern that was almost Hindu Indian in its complexity.

The unit, jelled into place with the first movement, slowed down to pick Kanoon up in the second section and stretched out from there.

Kanoon, never content to feel his way up and down old scales, frowned at the familiarity of his first notes, erased the memory of them with a succession of finely woven statements, profound commentaries on his state of mind and the deep regard he had for beauty and the Truth his instrument was capable of exploring.

The Gemini Lady's eyes glistened and the corners of her mouth grew moist as she listened-absorbed, each of his notes a precious piece of advice to her consciousness.

Kanoon fixed her mind with a soulful glance at the end of the piece and told her, telepathically, that he wanted her to follow him back to his dressing room.

The Gemini Lady, a lyrically constructed, Ethiopian-looking cocainist, her head held high, followed him, dazzled by the idea that she was going to be given the privilege of serving the master.

Warm applause and looks of approval followed them as they turned the far corner of the club, another kind of creativity about to happen.

Armandito stared up at the ceiling for a few seconds and lured the group off into a melodic guaguanco. His valentina to Kanoon.

Kanoon looked deeply into the almond-shaped eyes of the tall, dark-skinned Gemini Lady standing under the exit sign with him at the front door of the Pot.

"Why can't I spend the night, Kanoon?" he heard her ask through his cocaine, music soaked fog.

"Cause like I told you, baby...I don't like to spend the whole night with nobody. They think they own you when they spend the night."

The woman looked out sadly at the cold streets beyond the large, black picture window, and all around herself, at the uptilted stools and tables of the club.

"You sho is cold, Kanoon," she said softly.

He shrugged eloquently, denying nothing.

She leaned her lush pelvis into him and smoothly draped her arms around his slender shoulders.

"Why can't I stay a li'l while longer?" she cooed into his earringed ear.

"Number one, 'cause I don't want no mo', and number two, which is the most important, I got some work to do."

She withdrew her arms and stood back to take his full

126

measure, eyes narrowed, hands on hips.

"You know, they told me, when I first got on the scene, that you were a heartless, cold-blooded li'l black motherfucker, but I didn't know you were this...this..."

"Uhhh, good night, Justine."

She smiled a cool little smile at him as she stepped through the door into the cold air of the Pumpkin hour. "Good night, Kanoon," she replied, surrendering, and leaned back to kiss him once again.

"Be careful goin' to your car, baby," he cautioned her. "We got a bunch o' high crime rates hangin' 'round out there."

She laid a dazzling, sarcastic smile over her shoulder at him as she clutched her fur to her throat and tripped to the gun metal painted Porsche at the curb. She took the ticket on her windshield and ripped it into four neat pieces before jumping inside.

He stood in the doorway, freezing in his paisley caftan, and watched her zip away over patches of ice and tainted snow.

He closed the door, carefully rebolted, and strolled around the empty club aimlessly for a minute, winding up, finally, seated on the apron of the stage.

The Pot, my club, he bragged to himself. My club. Funny, he smiled in the dim light, how many different ideas circulate about how I wound up with this place. Some broad got it for me. The Mafia owns it. So and so owns a piece of it. I bet all them motherfuckers would shit a brick if they knew that this is righteously mine...bought with my own monies.

He sprawled back on the stage, laced his hands under his grimly tattered naps and stared at the fixtures in the ceiling for five thoughtful minutes.

Justine, goodbye, Justine. That sho was some beautiful coke you had Nancy, Luella, Mercedes, Donyale...God!

That broad must've been 6'9"! Branille, Hora, Tamu, Cleo, Margarite, Shirlean the dope fiend, Flavia... "Ooo Kanoon, you would love Rome, Rome would love you," Maureen, Darcye, Suzanne, Janine, Loretta, Nicca...ahhh Nicca, Graiela, Haitian voodoo lady, Toshiko...a koto person filled with grace note, La Na... "what's your real name?"

"That's it, my family name is Ba." Amy, Melba, Eartha, Katherine, Margo, Joan, yellow Birdeyes, Roberta, Lois, Coco, Erzulie, Otani from Osaka, Nina, Freda, Francine, Clotilde, Ingrid, Anouk, Jo Jo, Alice, Mozella, Madeline, Jakki, Lady, Bob Girl ("how hip do you want me to be?"), Stella, Barbara, Sherly, Veronica, Daisy, Pasha-Lustra ("I bankrupt myself each time we make love, Kanoon"), Maisha...beautiful Black Nubian Black woman...Aissha, Aissha

He cut off the litany of females he had slept with over the course of the last two years—those that had made an impression on him—by sitting up.

"Damn!" he mumbled, feeling the weight of his stiffened penis against his thigh. "Damn! I should've let the broad stay."

He sat up straight, trying to force his cocaine-induced erection away...Jacqueleen, Carla, Chanalo, Narali, Nra...discovered that it wasn't going to happen as long as his memory bank continued to function sensually, walked over to the bar, the front of his caftan jutting out like a Greek spear. Greek spear.

He looked up into the mirror behind the bar as he walked toward it, caught sight of the thumb piano beckoning to him from a chair on the bandstand.

Yeahhh, he spoke to the instrument and himself as he did an about-face and hopped onto the stand.

He stood looking down at the small half kidney-shaped box on the chair, at the flanged metal pieces over the hole, feeling his erection throb away as he did so.

He picked the instrument up with both hands, reverently, and sat down.

Looking out over the Twilight Zone atmosphere, gently plinking the instrument, the idea of what he felt he had to do suddenly dawned on him.

I got to get away...got to get away from all the broads, the dope, this terrible fast life I'm leading, the music I'm playing... "Concerto for Bassoon, Kanoon," echoed in his ear.

The Concerto shit! That's been done already, time to move on.

Why should that fuck with me, he's asked himself many times. Everybody wants to hear what a dude got made on. Duke Ellington would still have to play "Sophisticated Lady" or "Mood Indigo" or "Take the A Train" every now 'n then, if he were alive. God bless his beautiful soul. If Dolphy had lived, he might be getting requests for "Aggression." No telling what Bird would be asked to do.

He wandered up and down the scale, settling on certain patterns and then reversing them, a soulful, melodic refrain happening, playing *on* for the very first time, an instrument he had only been playing *at*.

Yeahhh...got to get away, his spontaneously composed tune said to him. Got to get off into Another Music. Yeahhh, Another Music.

The thought of it, coming to him so simply and directly, jammed both of his thumbs down on the metal flanges and held them there.

A Jazz Quartet for Thumb Piano.

He looked down at the box in his hands and felt tears spring to his eyes because he didn't know the African name for it.

Africa...yeahhh, Africa...that would be a good place to go get my shit together, get the Quartet together.

129

Yeahhh, Africa.

He stood, kissed the wooden box solemnly, replaced it on the chair and gracefully jumped from the low stage.

Yes suhhh, Africa— that's sho 'nuff where I need to go. Momma Africa.

Rhythms...Rhythms

"Chiiii-caaagoooo Deee-fenduhhh! Chiiii-caaagoooo Deee-fenduhhhh papuhhhh! Git yo' Chiiii-caaagoooo Deee-fenduh papuhhh!" "You gooooo to my headddd, you make my temperature rise...you go to my headddd...like a summer with a thousand Julys...you goooo tooooo my head..."

A sun-slashed day in 1947, Ruby Dee was doin' it in something called "Uncle Tom's Cabin," Countee Cullen was having a collection of his work whipped together, John Hope Franklin was getting off into our history, even then. Shirley Graham was doing beautiful things, Langston Hughes and Frank Yerby were gettin' down, each in his own way, and Jackie Robinson "broke" the color bar in big league baseball.

In July of the year, a Cancerian forever, even during bad times, in the Aquarian age, on a carefully spread out layer of newspapers, on a red and green checked tablecloth, the screeling, reeling, screeching, boiling, bubbling streets of Black Chicago's African westside, bobbing, weaving, dripping and bopping around outside. . . a baby, bald and wet, burst through his momma's tense, tender sweat, squinched his eyelids cynically at his neutral reception and thought "shiiii-it!"

"Turn the music back up, Lilah done had it, it's a li'l ugly boy." And then everybody laughed and was happy. A small place, a place without a decent view but staffed by love and feeling Black people.

Marlene dropped the pages lackadaisically from her hand onto the floor and turned to James. "James! James Wright Jr.! Are you sleep?"

"No, I am not, and I could really dig you not calling me James Wright Junior. 'Specially that Junior part, that has always bugged me for some reason."

James pulled his arm gently from under Marlene's head, twisted over to face her with a smile on his mouth, their faces moist from the warmth of the afternoon and their closeness.

Marlene Cole, dark nipples singing from the top of brown Fuji mounds, throat pulsing, lips brown, big, not full, big bow shaped, slender female arms slowly forming a cradle for her hands to lace themselves into a ten digit basket behind her skull cropped Afro.

"Alright," she answered, returning his smile as she gazed up at the ceiling, luxuriantly crossing her legs at the thigh, "Alright, I won't call you Junior, if it bugs you, but tell me something."

"Yeah, anything you want to know," he mumbled at her, as he reached across her breasts to pick up the ashtray on her side.

"Have you always wanted to write?"

James lit one of the half-smoked joints in the ashtray,

132

sucked up smoke and lay, holding it in and looking closely at Marlene's profile.

For a second, before he was aware that it was his own voice, he thought that the words were simply passing through his mind.

"I really love you, Marlene..."

She dropped her eyes, uncrossed her legs, stretched her arms out in front of her and reached over for the roach.

"That's not what I asked you," she said to him, avoiding the look in his eyes.

James, trying to cover his own surprise at what he'd just said, decided to be sincere, probably for the first time with a woman...not as a part of the New Game, Sincerity, but fo' real. "I'm hip to what you asked me...it's just that, well, I felt, I feel another kind of way and thought you should know about it."

"Just because we're in bed together and you think it's necessary."

"That's a helluva thing to say."

Marlene smiled slightly at the corners of her mouth, and passed the remains of the joint back to James, who took a quick, solid hit on it and dropped it in the ashtray.

"Why don't we start all over again, if it's gonna get complicated," she asked, pursing her mouth up for James to cut off the rest of her sarcastic statement by tonguing a chest full of good Jamaican smoke into it.

How long had it been, he thought carefully, as the smoke was slowly let out in thin streams from her nostrils. A week? Two? He reasoned, as they slowly, carefully fitted themselves together. Just two weeks...the first two weeks home, in the World, in June, back from all of those unpronounceable names, the snakes, fevers, booby traps, bullets, lonely, rainy nights, the stench of fish sauce, little almond-eyed people in black pajamas and conical hats, back from a yellow place trying to prevent, under the eternal white man's urgings, yellow men from having their own yellow government in their own yellow place...even if they were slightly more brown than yellow, and then his nerve endings began to ooze with a feeling that was so delicious that he felt his mouth begin to water.

Marlene Cole...unreal.

People in his family on the westside had warned him to be careful walking around the city after dark, something they'd always known him to do.

People in his family on the southside had also warned him...his Aunt Erma especially. "James Jr.! Thangs ain't the way they used to be, what with these gangs 'n stuff, shootin' that dope! They apt to snatch yo' head off out there!"

"Uh huh," he'd mumbled, he recalled with a smile, as the blood in the tiny veins of his eyelids gorged.

And then, walking around late at night, half wasted, he got jumped on by three young dudes and robbed...and then Marlene Cole. Too much.

It seemed so corny somehow, he thought, leaning up on his elbows to kiss Marlene's eyelids, her nose, and finally to press his mouth to hers, softly.

Fresh from 'Nam, nothing to do, really, no place to go, freshly bruised and ripped off, being asked to make a party with a couple old women lovin' partners, Slick Felt and Willie Fine, hip squares, but at the same time, streetologists into, but not practicing, the games they knew. The arguments they offered, over a fifth of Johnny Walker Black Label, were not so much dependent on logic as they were on passion.

"Looka'here, mannnnnn, they gon' have a bunch o' fine, fine sisters at this set...I mean fine! You hear me?! And well, heyyy, if you don't do nothin' else, you just might be able to pull your nuts up outta the sand. I know that yaller Vietnamese ass is becomin' just a hot memory by now."

"Yeahhhh," Willie Fine had added, always known for his "subtle" understatements, "you can see with your own eyes that the li'l motherfucker got 'bout three inches worth o' duck butter on his chest."

He had laughed with them, drank another three fingers of scotch, shaved close, slapped some French cologne on his jaws, got clean as the Board of Health, smoked two pinkie-sized joints in the bathroom, hoping that his mother wouldn't get home from her weekend visit to his sister's crib too soon, and was feeling very mellow when Felt and bruh' Fine picked him up, jokin' 'n signifyin'.

Marlene watched James' eyes glaze over as he slowly slid from off of her body, gently uncovering her breasts and belly to the warm afternoon air.

He lay, staring at the dappled sun patterns glowing on the pleated curtains for a long moment before she casually turned on her side, raising her firm brown thigh over and onto his stretched out lap. Playfully, seductively, the love that they had just made lazily sliding down across her lower thigh and smearing against his, she traced a half moon design on his hairless chest, puckered a tiny kiss in his ear and said, "You never did answer my question."

He smiled, in spite of the deep sexual fog he felt himself in...thoughts mumbling things in his consciousness about how good Black pussy really was, and is.

"Huh?," he answered, opening his eyes a slit's worth..."What question?"

Teasingly, "You sure do have a short memory."

"You don't do nothin' to help it get longer, and besides, how you gon' act? You lay up here and sling these big pretty legs all over me and then start asking questions. What kinda shit is this?"

They looked at each other, turning their faces toward each other so closely that they saw double, stared hard with semi-

135

serious expressions at each other, and then dissolved into incomprehensible giggles. The giggles melted into a shallow kiss, and then, the giggles dying into quiet, wordless moans, Marlene slid her thighs onto the outer edges of his thighs and began to roll her belly against his, slowly, rhythmically, lovingly. And the kiss grew deeper and deeper.

Have I always wanted to write? You motherfuckin' right I've always wanted to write, he answered her in his head, as his body explained to her body that they had not had enough of each other's feelings...either it was writing, exploring that kind of consciousness, trying to figure out a way to get rid of what the eminent streetologist, Iceberg Slim, has called "street poison," or so warm and soft, the heat of us and the middle of this tender afternoon...yeahhhhh, I've always wanted to write, niggers who've always wanted to write have always wanted to write, or murder somebody; to record with a conscience maybe, or scream, rant, rave, throw tantrums, bricks, molotov cocktails, ice picks, machetes, ball up fists, smash heads, try!...try goddammit! in some kind of way to say Something, if possible, about *our share*, the twenty-five dirty, slum slammed, rim shot, fucked up years of my time spent in this hypocritical, jiveass, white racist country they slaved us up into.

To try...ohhhhh my Lawwwwd Marlene...baby, you don't know how good you feel to me...to try and expose...noooo, don't come yet James, count to one thousand...think abstractly...about Chinese arithmetic maybe...to try and expose as many facets of what the real beauty of the Black Experience, as I have known it, has been, as well as the desperate richness of what our black asses have stooled onto, this beautiful place that these insensitive white folks beat the good Red Brother out of. And then tried to commit suicide in...with dumb dogmatism, smoke, fire, racism, bullshit and hypocrisy. Their bodies, coated now by

136

a moist down, fed, at last, by a single pulse, the sensation strengthened, built up by the weed from Montego Bay, spasmed together and then slowly relaxed...ebbed, flowed into a speechless, sexual catnap.

James, loving the feel of her body connected to, spread comfortably between his legs, circled her waist and crossed his hands onto her lush buttocks as she tried to roll over to his side. "Don't move, baby," he whispered in her ear, "don't move, you feel so good to me this way."

"Am I heavy on you?" she whispered back, after a light kiss on his neck.

"No," he answered, and felt something blaze up and melt inside him when he felt her small frame release its tension down the length of his body, her warm cheek nestled in the hollow of his throat.

Had it really been only two weeks?

He had no way of knowing, when he first saw her at the party...no way of knowing that they would ever get down to doin' it, and the idea that her lovemaking would be quiet, smooth, beautiful and profoundly passionate, no moans gleaned from movie closeups, no passion absorbed from any current book had ever occurred to him, and when it happened, when they first got off into it, the slow, deep, soulful welcome that he found in her left him walking around feeling a hunger for a woman's presence that he'd never felt before, a hunger that he felt the minute after they unlinked themselves.

The thought of them fucking each other into bad health had been discussed. "James, you know if this keeps up...I'm gon' wind up with a tilted womb or somethin'"...but they could never arrive at any sensible idea of what their love diet should be, so...they continued gorging themselves on each other, each taking the blame for wanting too much.

137

At the party, behind the prodding of Slick and Willie Fine, his only aim, with a head full of good smoke and three rum and cokes under his belt, was to run his li'l ol' game on the finest bitch on the scene and see if it would take him off into her bloomers. And then Marlene had eased in, with two other women, a small cocoa-hued Madonna wrapped in an Afrosari, a neutral, cool look in her eyes.

James, startled by something he felt in himself when he saw her, slyly placed himself in a position to watch her opening moves, the way she let herself get greeted, steered into and then momentarily neglected as the host and hostess trotted away to deal with the need for more ice cubes and beer.

He'd checked out her slightly disdainful look as she checked out the three white people who had been invited to the set, two women and one man, all three of them lurking around the fringes of things, marveling with their innocent eyes at the Black rhythm happening on the dance floor, and at the swiftness of the party drama that went up and down but never settled onto any plateau, nobody over in a corner discussing events of the day or intellectualizing themselves into absolute boredom.

As the party grew louder and more boisterous, he found himself more and more involved with the idea of wanting to find out who she was, because her style intrigued him, as well as the way her body was shaped.

"Felt, who's the li'l fine Black sister over there, the one with the..."

"Yeahhhh, yeahhhh, I dug her when she first came in. I don't know who she is...check with bruh' Willie."

"I already did, he doesn't know who she is either."

And there it stood, for a half hour of sipping, circling, trying to think of a sure-fire way to get his game off the ground, to try, somehow, to penetrate her rhythm, or what he thought her rhythm might be, to come in so strong that his vibes alone would kill off boyfriend, husband or whoever...because he felt she was exactly the woman for him. And after two more rum and cokes, he was certain of it.

He circled a group of dancers, paused to allow a would be rival time to warm the situation up and, the second the opportunity presented itself, he slipped in.

"Look,...my name is James Wright and...uh...I may as well be honest about it, I've been lookin' at you since you first walked in, tryin' to figure out what I could say to you. I mean, like, well, I think you're really a beautiful Black woman and..."

Marlene had turned away from him slowly, a vaguely sour expression on her face, leaving a slightly pissed and puzzled man behind her.

He spent a hot minute or two, letting the rum tell him what to do before he got control of himself, shrugged off his putdown and melted into the party, which, by this time, had grown even louder and more boisterous than before.

He had tried to take his frustration to other bodies, but for some reason, even though several of the bodies he shot at had better definitions, none of them turned him on in the way that she had done.

One of his targets, a middle-aged, smooth-skinned woman with granite features, fresh from the "society" page of the Black local weekly and loaded down with the smell of rich living, slid her tongue to the corner of his mouth as they danced and whispered in a creamy alto..."Your dick is just about to punch a hole in my thigh...don't you think we ought to do something about that, hummmmmmm?"

He eased out of her grasp at the end of the record, feeling uneasy with her aggressiveness.

And then the other one, the slightly plump, pretty-faced brown chick, fresh out of college...who wanted to talk (after

139

Willie had told her, putting her on) about what it had been like to be in Vietnam, in the Wahhh.

James cut a dirty look at Willie Fine passing by, on his way to the killin' flo' with a young fox, and received a casual shrug in reply...and turned to speak, in quick, jerky sentences, to the brown collegian for a few minutes.

A few minutes was all he could take, not of the young woman, but of the bad, bad vibes caused by a discussion of something he'd hated to be a part of, the U.S. Army in Vietnam.

He excused himself as soon as it seemed polite to do so, picked up somebody's drink and wandered out onto the back porch...past a couple belly rubbing in the hallway, oblivious to everybody, and three brothers trying to talk one of the white chick's bloomers off in the kitchen.

He stood, leaning on his elbows on the banister, smoking a cigarette, sipping on what happened to be cheap wine, and smiled sarcastically at the desperate little green plants clinging to sticks that seemed to be stuck in concrete.

"Back in the World," they used to say to each other in 'Nam,..."when I get back out in the World...I'm gon' do this, or that," away from the jungle and the monsoons and everything.

"So, this is the World," he said to himself as the sound of B.B's "Lucille" twanged in his ear, coupled to all the tonal pitches of Black laughter. "The World," he spoke to himself again, drained the cup and stared up at the irregular shapes surrounding him on the back porch, first floor, of someone's apartment on 71st Street, deep in the heart of Chicago's southside.

Some premonition made him feel her presence before she spoke...or had it been her perfume? A light, cool smell that drifted past his nose and back to it. He had a quick, crazy vision pass through his head the second before he knew who

140

it was...of the two of them being pulled through the sky by a comet trailing bright green bits of fire from its tail.

"'Scuse me, would you happen to have a...?"

Be cold, he had reminded himself, as he turned to face her in the shadows, the noise bursting through the door behind them both, be cold, but instead he'd fumbled in his pockets like a nervous schoolboy, and when he cupped his hands to light her cigarette, his hands were trembling from the wrists down.

"Ohhh," she'd said, recognizing him and then took a couple drags on her cigarette and turned to go back inside.

"Can I ask you a question before you cut out...again?" made her pause, and turn around.

"Why not? Ask."

"Well, first of all, you don't have to tell me why you walked away from me earlier...if you don't want to."

"O.K., I won't."

"But," he added quickly, playing for time, "it sure would be a groove if you did."

"I thought you said I didn't have to if I didn't want to."

The cursing at her was internal, but the cutting edge of what he'd felt most definitely had come through.

"Look, Miss Lady, why don't we both stop jivin'...I want to know why you walked away from me. Did I say something to bug you?"

She had studied him for a long moment...

"Look,...uh...?

"James, James Wright...what's yours?"

"Marlene Cole."

"Marlene, come on over here and sit on the steps with me, unless you're afraid to get your dress dirty or something."

Her look had been the acceptance of a challenge; they walked to the edge of the porch and perched on the worn,

141

wooden steps.

"O.K., now, what were you gon' say? Would you like another drink? I could go inside and cop something."

"No," she answered, and checked him closely, as though making certain of who she was dealing with, "I'm not that much of a drinker. Do you smoke?"

"Yeahhhh, but I'm not holdin'."

The joint she dipped down into her bra for was fat, well rolled and filled with dynamite.

They found themselves automatically strolling down into the "back yard," a few yards of patioed concrete stuffed behind a wooden fence, they leaned against the fence, passing the joint back and forth, the veins in James' temple popping with the good feeling of being off alone with the one of his choice.

"O.K., now, go on, rap to me..."

He could see the slight curls form around her mouth, something he would come to know well, as she started in, releasing a slow stream of smoke.

"Let me put it this way. To begin with, it might have been a little unfair of me to put you in a bag the minute you opened your mouth, but that's what I did."

James stood, studying her profile in the half light spilling over onto them from the back porch window, people moving back and forth inside throwing shadows on her smooth cocoa-colored skin.

"You put me in a bag, huh?"

"I'd already made up my mind, before we walked in the door, the first dude who comes up to me with that 'you really a beautiful Black woman' stuff, I'm gonna walk away from."

James, loaded, smiling crookedly, found himself on the defensive, infighting, "But you *are* a beautiful Black woman."

Marlene sighed impatiently and cocktailed the roach,

waited for a light and took a deep hit before passing it on.

"I know I'm a beautiful Black woman. I knew it a long time ago because my grandfather sat me on his knee and told me, and my grandmother and all my uncles, and my mother and my father."

"Hold on! Wait a minute! I mean, like, well, what's your objection to bein' told...!"

"Nooooo! You hold on a minute! Don't get me wrong, don't think I don't dig it. It's just that, well, to my mind, a lot of brothers sound like they're talkin' to a magazine cover when they say..."

James found himself laughing uncontrollably, unable to explain why, but knowing that she understood and then, as though it had been rehearsed, they went through a series of bits culled from here and there, made a litany of them...

James started it off with..."Black queen, where have you been all my life?"

And she followed up with, "Whasss happenin', pretty sister?"

"Uh huh, looka'here, Momma!"

"What is it, dark sugar?"

"Been lookin' for you, Miss Beautiful Midnight."

'Til they got down to..."Uh dig Sistuh Essence...I got some words for you." And they both cracked up.

"Now then, Black brother, after all these cliches have been shot at you, you're supposed to be swept off your feet. And if you haven't been, well, you just might be called some other, different kinds of names, from another time, can you dig where I'm comin' from?"

"I hear you, baby. I hear you."

"I mean, don't you think we should expect to hear a li'l bit more than what the current rhetoric is tellin' folks to say?"

They stopped giggling and stared at each other seemingly for the first time, the noise of the party and the people a long

143

way off.

"Yeahhh, I guess you're right," he answered, seriously, "but I don't give a fuck what you say...I *still* think you're a beautiful Black woman and that ain't no rhetoric."

Her eyes dropped shyly as a slow piece of music filtered out to them, dropped in on their high. He reached for her, placed both arms around her waist as they swayed, in time to the music, suddenly a million miles from everywhere and everyone. Had it only been two weeks? For so much to have happened it seemed longer, not in terms of days but months, and in terms of Happenings.

Riding home in Slick Felt's big, black ride, after a light, tender kiss and a promise, comparing notes and feelings about the fine chicks they had both shot at, James felt very groovy and secure with Marlene's telephone number scribbled on a matchbook cover safely pushed down into his shirt pocket.

And, like flashes of life spinning around in front of him, the luck of finding, the following Monday, a small, tastefully furnished apartment in Hyde Park...Afro-Danish, he'd thought, as the landlady pointed to the fireplace that didn't work, but was there, in effect, for the effect.

The landlady's feelings went out to him as he counted out June, July and August in her hand, plus the hundred and twenty-five dollars "security" payment.

His only thought had been of how beautiful it would be to lay up on his ass for three months, 'til his saved-up Army money began to thin out...and to have Marlene.

"James?" a voice coming from somewhere, soft and lazy. He smiled indulgently as he turned to her and cradled her head in the hollow of his neck, loving the smooth feel of her softness.

"I know, you don't have to tell me, you're hungry."

"Unmm huhn."

"Well," with mock seriousness, "git up 'n get on yo' job! I got some bacon and eggs in the box...fix me something too, while you're at it...I feel a li'l snackish myself."

She kissed his chin and slid out of bed. Watching her small, hourglass-shaped figure glide away to the bathroom, he thought casually about the early days of their relationship.

He suspected that she had pushed a little shit off into the game after he had called her five times in two days and had gotten no answer, and, when he finally reached her...the conversation seemed to have had more strain on it than there should have been, in view of the kind of vibes they had go on between them at the party.

He eased up off of the stacked mattresses on the floor and put Hubert Laws on the portable, slid back down onto the bed, and back into his memory...

"Remember, we sat, we talked out in the yard while the rest of the people jumped up and down inside...we talked...and you told me about yourself, a li'l...and I told you..."

Too coldly, she'd answered..."Ooo, yes, I remember...I've been kind of busy."

"Well, dig, what I wanted, I mean, what I wanted to ask you is whether or not you wanted to catch Pharoah Sanders. He's opening at the Brownshoe tonight."

Jive bitch, I'll bet she's layin' up with some other nigger right now, he had thought bitterly, patiently waiting for her to tell him whether or not he was going to have the pleasure of her company for that evening.

When she finally said, "I guess you'll want me to pick you up...unless you want to bus it," his day had been filled with all sorts of tensions.

He had wandered around his apartment drinking sweet wine, scribbling three-line poems and rehearsing what he wanted to say to her that evening.

145

As he lay sprawled out, staring up at the ceiling, the slow, warm memory of how much he had wanted to do it to her aroused him slightly.

Her aloofness, which really wasn't that, or at least not in the way he had ever experienced it with any other woman, showed him a kind of private privacy that wouldn't allow him to grab her as he had planned to do when she strolled into his apartment.

"Nice little place...really nice," she mumbled as she moved around and sprawled gracefully into the corner of the sofa.

He smiled at the thought of all the fumbling around he'd done, trying to be supersuave.

"Uh, I have a li'l juice, if you'd like to sip on something before we cut out."

Her reply had been eloquent. She pulled two more of her custom rolled joints from her bra and held them both out to him.

"I told you before...I'm not too much of a drinker...a friend of mine laid these on me...they've got hash ground up with the weed, 'sposed to be pretty good. I haven't had any yet."

And that's the way it had gone down; she, full of surprising twists and turns right before his very eyes. At just that point where he would be about to form one definite notion about her, she would suddenly become something else, in the most literal sense of the word.

They got mellow and went to see Pharoah, floated it seemed through the dark, dappled forests of Washington Park, stopped for a kiss near the lagoon, wove in and out, eased the long way 'round to the Drive and down along the lakefront listening dreamily to "My Favorite Things," his right hand moving over to rest gently on her silky brown thigh.

146

"Your hand is on my thigh," she'd said to him, a hint of coldness in her voice.

"I know," he replied, in a low, clear voice. And then she placed both of her hands on his hand and held them there 'til they wheeled up through the garish lights of Old Town...smiling and making native city jokes about the tourists.

"James! How do you want your eggs?"

The voice from the kitchen jarred him for a second...so deep in his thoughts...damn! You'd think a woman would know how a man liked his eggs, after practically living together for two weeks. "Once over lightly, baby!" he called back to her.

It had been one of those nights when everything in life was happening right, right down to stumbling across a parking space only two blocks from the set.

To be out in the streets with a pretty woman, pockets fairly deep, a hip-looking bunch of well-coordinated clothes on your back, feeling good and seeing and being seen by all the rest of the fast people out there.

And Pharoah had been out of sight! After he had "played" finger piano, sounding bowl, bead strung Indian bells and soprano and tenor sax...he blew some more because his own group hadn't heard enough...*and* sang.

The good feeling, his arm around the back of her seat, stylin', staring soulfully into her eyes from time to time by the light of candles, wanting to fuck, wanting the pussy so badly that he felt himself throbbing with the urgency, but, after the set, after the warmth and the groove they found themselves in, the urge to make love and not simply screw hit him and it was right there, at that point, that he knew he was in a fight for his independence, because only chumps, suckers, pootbutts and squares fell in...couldn't even say it, just couldn't.

147

Marlene swayed into the bedroom, a towel saronged around her body, a tray with two plates of bacon 'n eggs, toast and coffee on it.

"What're you layin' up here lookin' all dreamy about?" she asked him, a familiar, sarcastic looking tilt on her smiling mouth. She had caught him drifting, once again, back and forth, in and out. And, once again, he felt, for some reason he couldn't quite pin down, that he should feel resentful of this invasion of his private privacy but he couldn't force the feeling to stick. They ate, mumbling to each other between bites.

"You know...I was just thinking about this novel I'm off into...any mo' bacon? I feel like I'm starving to death!"

"Not done...you want some more?"

"I could, really...you know how that weed jacks your appetite up and..." with a sly smile at her upper thigh..."besides."

"O.K.,...you don't have to explain...three or four pieces?"

"Four would knock me out."

She smiled cutely over her shoulder at him, as she tightened the towel up under her armpits and eased away to the kitchen.

..."Another Place!" That's what I'll call it! That's all the damned thing needed was a title...yeahhhh..."Another Place"...I better start on it again...sometime this week or else I'm not going to...period...guess that means I'll have to drag my ass out of bed one of these days.

He smiled into his cup, listening to the bacon sizzle and thinking of how hip Marlene was about his writing. She didn't think it was weird or anything that he should be writing a novel, after he'd confessed to her that the only things he'd ever had published were two poems in his high school paper...and a short story in *Soul Digest*. He gently set his coffee cup down, leaned back on his pillow and sighhhed

148

deeply...Marlene...

After their night out, after Pharoah, she parked, looked him in the eye and asked, coolly, quietly, "Well,...aren't you going to invite me up?"

The first night had been a dream. Even the thought of it, this much later in time, made his thighs quiver with nervousness...the memory of not being able to have an erection...the sweat and frustration, her calm understanding, and finally the warmth, the terrible softness of her smooth dark skin glistening in a shaft of chalky moonlight...of all things, on a night of a full moon...it had been UNreal.

They had made love for hours, or so it had seemed, joined sometimes by him in her, at other times by a kiss that held their mouths glued together for so long that their lips became tender from the pleasure.

It was perfect, James felt, except that the whole situation prevented him from seeing other women and writing, and especially now that she had practically moved in, that is, if birth control pills in the medicine cabinet meant anything...but it really wasn't her fault, he reasoned out, not about the writing anyway. She even encouraged him to write, but how? When would he have the time? If they jumped into bed and stayed there, from the time they met 'til the time they parted...at one-thirty or so, because she had to punch the clock at two-thirty.

He lay back, his neck crooked up in his pillow, a slow burp wallowing up, watching Marlene step into, pull her clothes on. He never felt ready for her naturalness in front of him, the way she leaned over to pull on her stockings, the slight roll of pear belly flesh curling up around her sides as she leaned this way or that, and the occasional sight of the dark petals of her vagina as she gracefully propped her foot up on the chair to pull her panty hose up.

"Marlene?"

"Huh...what?"

"Do you really have to go to work today?"

She stood in the center of the small living room, looking distractedly into the fireplace that didn't work, and then into his eyes, a beautiful dark vision in canary yellow and mint green. "James...baby, I'm runnin' late now...and I've already gotten two write-ups in the last week for being late."

A quick kiss, a roaming rub up both sides of her waistline, the feverish urge to want to get off into it again.

"James!" urgently. "I have to go, baby!"

"Will I see you tonight after you get off?"

"Why don't you pull on some clothes and run me to work, keep the car and pick me up tonight?"

The frown on James' face clearly indicated his reluctance to leave his crib to dash down to the post office.

"Uhh huh...just as I thought...ol' lazy bones!"

"Well,...uh...that's beside the point...will I see you...?"

"Mmmmm,...I don't know, James...my mother is beginning to act kind of funny, like, hey,...I'm a grown woman and everything but I still live at home and this I'm-spending-the-night-with-my-girlfriend stuff is wearing thin."

Momma'll be thinkin' you kinda sweet on your girlfriend, huh?"

"Hahhh hahhh...I doubt it...but I think I better make it on in tonight. Why don't you give me a ring tomorrow morning...say about ten? Maybe we can get together and do something."

A fake leer, another kiss, a longer one this time..."Don't work too hard," and then a softly blown kiss from the door...closed, nothing, alone.

He wandered through his apartment, checking the neat way she'd left the kitchen, strolled into the bedroom and replaced Hubert Laws with Eric Dolphy, flopped back down on his

150

mattresses and fingered around in the ashtrays for enough of a roach to smoke, found one, lit up and laid back scratching lackadaisically in his pubic hairs.

His head went to the top drawer of his dresser, to the six hundred dollars he had there and to what he would have to do when he got down to half of it.

"Get a job," was the second thing his mother had said, after checking him out carefully for lost limbs and foul habits, and stuffing sweet potato pie into his jaws, grateful that her only son had returned safely.

"Hurry up and get a job!" his father had said, sitting on the edge of a lumpy bed, in a dim, roach-infested room...and had slyly conned him out of a twenty, after asking, "How's yo' Momma doin', boy? I been meanin' to get over and see her...but,...well, you know how it is after you bust up...and we been apart so long now that we ought to file for a divorce."

To his mother, trying to tie him back to her apron strings, the only thing he could say was, "Momma, look, I've been through a heavy number, Vietnam was no playground...I want to lay out awhile and get myself together."

To his father, there was nothing to say, the sad state of where he was overwhelmed them both, nothing to say, but several things to do. First, an apartment, a place where he could do his own thang, which he was prepared to take his time about finding, and then the unexpected, Marlene! which gave him a new urgent reason to have a place.

He slid off of the rumpled bed, a little high, and yawned his way into the kitchen, nibbled on the crust of a piece of toast and strolled back into his bedroom, rubbing his belly and thinking of Marlene and his novel.

He threw himself, stomach down, onto the mattresses and lit a cigarette, twisted over onto his back, stared absently at the ceiling for a few minutes, his mind whirling from the

151

sounds of Eric Dolphy to Marlene to what Saigon had been like, to...to...got up suddenly and walked over to his notebook and pencil, returned to the bed, re-lit the roach and began to toke up and to scribble... "The slirred, slurred hints of Eric Dolphy, Hubert Laws, Albert Ayler, Bird, Virgil Phumtee...alias Abschlom Ben Scholomo, Jutta Hipp, Pharoah...yes Allah, Pharoah, Son-sun Ra, Toshiko Mariano, Coltrane and Miles, Alice knows something transcendental...bless her melodic soul...cool doin's from Cecil Taylor, Armando Peraza and Billy Mitchell...tainted smoke from singed, center cut po'k chops, three-day-old catfish grease, six-day-old chicken grease, Nigroid farts from red beans, black-eyed peas and limas...black foot roaches with pregnant pouches burning in twisted cones of flaming Defender papers...'Chiiii-caaagooooo Deee-fen-duuhhhh!'...bar-be-cued ribs, hic'kry smoked, fried snow balls, hip games run on the heart...all kinds of smelly shit, Miles Davis sketching Spain...Saeeta.

"Art Blakely, messenger. Blackniss zigzagging into skag...too bad, sad...Junky of the Year, closed doors, a shootin' gallery, harm done that can never be undone, slums, flushing toilets, doo doo dropped from four floors above, the rank smell of things. Racism, the slavemaster's obscene defense of his li'l pink pecker...Western Anglo-Saxonism. Dig it?

"Days and nights."

He paused, his neck cramped from bending over the notebook, lit the end of another roach, burned his thumb and forefinger as he sucked the last smoke down, placed what was left back into the ashtray and lapsed off into a five minute nap.

"Too much happening," he continued writing after the pause...

"Too much happening...no time to sleep...even the most

152

ordinary sounds bring us music bounced off of steel flecked clouds, days and nights of endless blacks and whites, endless blacks, endless whites...Thank God for Atheism...drum thunderbeats from the streets, the pigs steadily pushing...why is there a Shaft?...well, o.k....maybe Everything really is Everything."

James stopped scribbling, the high of what he felt cancelling out, erasing the other crazy urges he felt like wandering off into, for no reason that he had a reason for...God! He thought suddenly...how I love this bitch!

He squashed the page he had been writing on into a ball and threw it across the room...shit!...and started on a fresh page, stopped, missing the sound of music, went over to put Nancy Wilson, Lady Day and Roberta Flack on and returned to his work, feeling in tune.

"And then, in the middle of the afternoon," he started, "after love's skirrrlings and post-hypnotic sex naps, bacon, eggs, toast, coffee, dancing in place, trying to make sense, some kind of sense out of no-sense, wanting to be the first Black Zen choirboy, really."

James looked down at his fingers wrapped around the pencil and the movement of both of them as though they didn't belong to him...stared at the shadows pouring down onto his curtains and continued..."Nights cancelled by diamond-flecked stars...music from a bunch of lyrically stringed guitars, Black ghosts with shiny faces, full of life, despite slavery's pressures, tangled up in Mystory, not history."

James paused, frowning, slammed the notebook shut and asked himself..."What the fuck am I doin'?"

He slowly lay back and thought about how much a part Marlene was beginning to play in his life...forced the thought of her from his mind and sat back up to write...

"Miles ahead, cool breezes, God in His Heaven, the Devil

in His Hell, all the rest of Us in Between, our ears snatched up by, raped with noise of rumbling trains...screeching plans, our noses heated up and opened by unusual smells and feelings...some of them so heavy that a Mack truck could be driven through afterwards.

"Never on Sunday, 'Sunday is a good day for Crucifixion,' Swiss Von Vernon the Third once said, but any day can be Friday, with a stick of good herb, a willing, joy blown cunt, some good music, the long hot taste of a honey browned nipple...soul food for real...and the thought of more to come...

"To come...to come...another dimension..."

He came to..."another dimension"...stumbled around in his brain for something to follow it with, couldn't find anything, slammed his notebook closed, threw his pencil against the far wall and groaned, "Who in the fuck would buy some fucked up shit like this!?"...and began to search around in his disordered closet for something to get out into the streets in.

Forty-seventh Street, from Lake Park to State Street, walking slowly into Friday night on the near southside, eyes taking it all in, peeling the fronts of the buildings back like banana skins, slowing down to recall, remember.

He and the dude almost passed each other without recognition, but they turned, each of them with a mouthful of greetings.

"Heyyyyy mannnnnnn, where you been keepin' yo'self? Damn! I ain't seen you in...what? Two, three months?"

"What's happenin', Rookie? Been longer 'n that. I just got back." Rookie, bent around the shoulders, trying to look healthy but failing, compassion flexing the muscles in a face racked by Jones.

"Ohh yeahhhh," a hip crook of the neck, a knowing slant

154

to the lips. "How much time did you have to do? I just got out...myself."

"Nawww man, I ain't been doin' no time. Well, not exactly, but I guess, in a way it was. I got drafted, man, shipped off the streets and shot over into the 'Nam."

"Awwww, I thought...hah hah hah, yeahhhh, I dig it now, the other pigs got hold o' you."

"Never thought about it that way, but I guess that's 'bout the way it was."

"Yeahhhh, well, that's the way that be, sometimes. You lookin' good, I'll say that. Uhh, dig, I got to get on, got to get on over here and take care this business, you dig? Good seein' you again, man, good seein' you."

James strolled on, turning sadly to watch his old high school buddy do his junky shuffle down the street, threadbare pants shining across his buns like a new nickel.

Poor old Rookie...same age I am and look at him, motherfucker looks older than white paint. God! How that li'l Black bastard used to play shortshop! And now look at him. Too bad he didn't have a chance to make it to 'Nam, with all that pure shit over there he'd really be into a thang.

He shuffled a bit himself, subconsciously falling into the hip, boppish, knee-dipping step that stamped a dude with a street presence. Forty-seventh Street stretched out before him, at Woodlawn, like a mass of twisted wires, snaggle-toothed buildings, hazy and blurred, oily with the colored faces of the black people who came and went in every color.

Well, I'll be goddamned! It looks like her, walks like her.

"Pearline!? Pearline Dawson!?"

"Yeah!? Who!? Well! if this ain't!...James Wright! Where you been keepin' yourself?"

James smothered the six-month-old page of his teenaged passion in his arms, more for old time's sake than immediate desire...stretching out from the shoulders a bit to get around

155

the bulk of what had once been a slender young sister.

"This must be my day, I just ran into Rookie down the street."

"Shiiii-it! That ain't no news. I see Rookie all the time, with his thievin' ass. You know he's on dope now."

"Yeahhh,...I checked him out."

A long, hot pause drew their eyes together and the memory of all the afternoons they'd walked home from school together, stopped in funky hallways and swapped juicy kisses spiced with bubble gum, candy corn and Spanish peanuts, pulled their bodies together, as if drawn by magnets.

"What're you doin' for yourself now? You know I haven't seen you since...since..."

"Well,...uh...the last time we were together," and he emphasized *together*, "was in 1990."

"O wowww! 1990...I guess I was still a wild-eyed female then, huh?"

"No wilder than all the rest of 'em," he replied with a sultry wink.

"Well, that's beside the point anyway. What's been happenin' with you since then?"

James stared at his old girlfriend for a hard second, wondering what she would say to him if he suggested, as he felt like doing, that they go off somewhere and do what they used to do, but thought better of it. "What's been happenin' with me? Ooo, I been doin' my thang, or rather, I was doin' my thang 'til I got drafted. I just got home a couple weeks ago and right now I ain't doin' shit. I thought I'd lay out for about a month, check out the scene, see how many of my old girlfriends still love me."

"James, you still talkin' all that jive. Well, I guess I won't be one of 'em, one of those old girlfriends. I got three girls now and, I hope, a boy on the way."

"O com' on, Pearline, you ain't pregnant? You don't look

156

pregnant.''

''I guess I don't look it, not with all this excess weight I'm carryin', but I'm 'bout three months gone now.''

James winked, all of his stops out now, remembering, more strongly all the time, how wild and free their thing had been.

''Three months, huh? Must be pure jelly now.''

Pearline flashed her eyes coyly, ''James! You oughta be 'shamed of yourself.''

James' mind, roving all over the street, suddenly taking itself past the conversation he was having, knowing that it would eventually have him punching Pearline's tough-shit card, settled on one thought as he absently brushed his mouth along Pearline's cheek in parting...wonder what the hell Marlene will look like in a year? Two, three years?

''Hey baby, you know I was just jokin', you know I wouldn't be tryin' to break up a happy home.''

Pearline looked at him directly, straight. ''You don't have to worry 'bout nothin' like that. You know me and Leroy never got married. You remember Leroy Dillens, don't you?''

James nodded casually, the picture of a tall, vulture-necked dude with a cap in the top row of his teeth flashed through his mind.

''Yeah, baby, yeahhh, I remember Leroy. Is that...?''

''He was. We thought we was gon' have somethin' beautiful go on but, well, you know how things go down sometimes. He lost his gig, started hangin' out, tryin' to be nickel slick, with a bunch of ol' jiveass thug type niggers, got popped...and...well, anyway, he's up at Statesville now. Uh, why don't you take my number? I'm home just about every evenin'.''

James fumbled around in his pocket for a stray card, a piece of paper, handed it to Pearline and watched her

157

carefully scrawl her name, address and phone number on it.

As she scribbled, he carefully, almost studiously, worked his way from her feet to her head, and decided, after a quick, careful checking out, that she was already an old woman. She couldn't have been any older than he was, he reasoned out, after all, he had been a junior when she was a sophomore. Wowww, you leave the scene for a bit and when you trip back in, from wherever, the people you've grown up with, maybe loved, like Pearline, look like they've been slapped in the face by six hundred hands in ugly gloves, swinging a stick with gnat shit on the end of it. He took the scribbled-on piece of paper, and made a mental note to get rid of it as soon as possible.

"You be sure 'n get in touch with me, James, o.k.?"

The bitch is looking for somebody to feed those crumbcrushers, never happen...umh huhnn.

"Yeah baby, sure will, and it won't be too long. I wouldn't want to dent the li'l guy's head."

Her flushed up, wobbly way of looking over his shoulder told him it was still there, that he could always cop, and it brought down a groovy, tender warmth between them, this heavy, lascivious, honest flirting that would, or could, take them off into a heavy, dramatic sex session anytime they chose to have it happen.

"I bet I won't hear from you."

"I bet you will," James sang in her ear, as he brought himself in close and then eased off, the lump in her belly making him feel uncomfortable.

"I'll be seein' you, Pearline, be good and don't be doin' anything I wouldn't do."

Pearline threw a dry little wave with her fingers his way as they split, "I've already done it, believe me, baby. Momma has already done it. You take care...and don't forget, I'll be expectin' to hear from you."

Pearline, a body from yesterday, suddenly out of sight, out of mind...but not really. Old friends, Pearline, acquaintances. Rookie, dudes from the block, any number of people roaming up and down, dudes from yesterday, still doing the same old number in front of the joints, neon signs flickering already, at twilight. Come. Come. Come.

Crossing Drexel Boulevard.

Crossing Drexel Boulevard and looking back over his right shoulder at what used to be Sutherland Lounge.

The Sutherland Motel and Lounge. The Lounge, Miles blowing in a single blue spot of light that shimmered on the bell of his horn like liquid fire; Diz, secure in his nationalistic feelings, jiving, saying with himself, his art, goddamn folks! Don't take it *too* seriously, life is just a bit of triple tonguing...Sarah...Sassy...Dinah...Brassy...another time...lush evenings filled with southside ain't-nobody-here-but-us-niggers drama, the kind of drama that was never called that, just...it-was-Saturday-night.

He hopped up onto a bench, on the dividing greenery between the east and the west side of the street, ignoring the stares of two resident winos and a duo of irritated, frowning white cops wheeling by.

The Sutherland. How many nights? How many times had he taken a woman to the Sutherland, choked up, kicks gleaming, head smoky, out for the evening, fox in hand, being fed smooth game and soulfully persuaded.

The night he ran into his father, sitting across the horseshoe-shaped bar...a Polynesian princess on the left, a Viking broad on the right .. sittin' 'n sippin', loaded back. They nodded and let the unsaid remain unsaid.

I wonder if I've seen too much, he asked himself, peeking out of the corner of his eyes at the winos, their legs draped, folded neatly across each other, their heads forming a natural triangle as they leaned into each other.

159

Been into too many bags, he mumbled to the winos and leapt from the bench, too many bags for me to be sitting here, going through these kinda changes.

On the northwest corner of Cottage Grove, where his walking seemed to become dreamlike...filled with soft, oozing thoughts of Mildred and Wilma. The bitch married Buster...hmf! And Milly and I didn't fuck 'til after she'd had a fuckin' baby by an albino and done a bit in the slams, and even then, even then, it was quick and on the floor.

James smiled on his way into the liquor store, "the one kind of store you can always be certain will be open in a Black neighborhood," bought a pint of cheap pluck, paused in the toilet of the dingy poolroom a few doors down the street and slopped a few, long gulps down his throat.

Afterwards, strolling nonchalantly from the poolroom, the hum of the street seemed clearer as he walked it. The sound of Charlie Parker, legend and musician, blowing "Mama Inez" from someone's window, from the genius of Charlie Parker #6..."Fiesta"...Charlie Parker and his South of the Border Orchestra...jammed him into place, locked his knees, 'til the album swang to an end with "My Little Suede Shoes."

Bird...Bird...whewwwwww...

Another dude who'd been jammed into place, a heroin user, nodded sympathetically to James as they passed each other on 47th Street, in the ghetto, understanding what he had blown...what they'd just felt and heard.

James passed on, nodding...remembering the pressures Bird had laid on so many people...not just fellow musicians, but spiritualists, dope addicts, white women and their mommas, neutral avant gardists, waiting for a Messiah without nasty habits and music-crazed ladies who had run up and down the scale too often...the humming of the street became even clearer as he walked it, as high and fucked up

160

as anyone else lounging around in the warmth of the late afternoon, or nursing their pains with companions suffering from the same diseases.

Things haven't changed...he thought, hesitating close to a bunch of high-voiced men, laughing at a joke that he had not heard, but had understood, from the sounds of their loose laughter. Things really haven't changed...the fluid, swiveling character of the streets, filled with as many games..."Hey man, have you ever seen a watch like this?!"...as there were people in the streets who were willing and ready to run games...sang in his head as he felt his way to State Street.

Snatches of all kinds of music, music mixed with ouds, kanoons, and blow torches sang at him, slid into and past his ears, like heavy splashes of hot texture...

The texture of niggers. That moisturized, smoothly sculptured sister with the deep mahogany skin and the teakwood riffles in her hair walking...no...sailing away in front of me...sure would like to do a piece on that..."the texture of niggers"...that's what I'll call it..."the texture of niggers"...that would have to be the hippest, richest piece of shit ever done in America...the oil of our faces, how our women look, what kinds of sounds we make as we laugh, how weird our intellectuals are, our artists, what and how incredible our welfare mothers are, our mothers, period. Why, and for what reasons we drink too much, and buy too much and...yesss...probably it's good to be oversexed...sorry 'bout that, conservative niggers!

And our paranoia, our own special paranoia..."if you do this you ain't a brother...and, if you do this, you are a brother..."

"Where is yo' head, mannnnnn?"

"Whatchu mean? Where is my head,...mannnnnn?"

"Looka'here, motherfucker!"

161

"Hey mannnnnn, don't call me that, I don't dig it. I'm a cocksucker!"

"Right on!"

"Where's yo' consciousness, nigger?!"

"Uhhhh...uhhhhhh..."

"Uhhh...huhum...dig it! You ain't shit!"

"Right on!..."

Snatches of music, always, no dull suburbs in the inner city, a no-no, not allowed, too much noise...

I sure would like to do a piece...call it "Sketches of the Ghetto"...a thang Gil could never orchestrate...but what the hell! Who knows? Show a motherfucker who knows a li'l taste about music and who knows what might happen?

Snatches of music...Aretha, Donny, Roberta, Billie, Muddy, Bessie, Ravi, vocal, verbal, hostile, warm, Latin, Eastern, Northern, Southern...slipped past his ears, stuck in them, like structures born of black clay, like splashes of dark texture.

"The Texture of Niggers," he thought excitedly, "The Texture of Niggers"...that would sho' 'nuff have to be the hippest piece ever done on niggers in America...

A white bum, a derelict from other times lurched out of an alley, his face grizzled, his body slack.

"'Scuse me, Mister...would you happen to have any spare change?"

James felt an immediate, rank hostility well up inside him.

"Sorry, but don't you know that niggers have never had any spare change?"

The bum swayed slightly..."None? Not even a couple pennies?"

"Not since your great grandfather did his number on our Black asses."

The bum stopped swaying, balanced himself with difficulty and stared at James with intense puzzlement...seemingly

162

unable to cope with what was being said to him.

Finally, seeing that he was not likely to get any spare change, he patted James on the forearm with a distant, absentminded touch and stumbled back up into the alley.

James resisted the wild impulse to run up behind the bum and kick him...decided instead, with a smile at his vicious thinking, to stop in a nearby hallway for a leak and to cushion the heat in his belly with a few more swigs on his bottle.

He was mildly surprised after he had swallowed a few times to discover, pulling the bottle out of the brown bag in the dimly-lit hallway, that it was three quarters empty..."O wowwwwww," he muttered softly...

Leaning against a corner of the hallway, he tilted the bottle up with one hand and held himself, patiently, waiting for his bladder to push itself, and finally when it happened, the spray of his stream caused him to bring the bottle down and watch the arch of his urination as it splattered into the already piss-stained corner.

Just like the old days, drinking cheap wine and pissing it out in stinky hallways...and goddammit!...on my shoes! The old days...when was that? When I was fifteen? He drained the corner of the bottle and carefully placed it in the corner he'd just pissed in, eased out of the hallway and continued walking, the flood of cheap wine warming his stomach, fuzzing his mind.

In the old days there had been a Shirley, a Barbara, a Doris, a Pearline and, once, a Myrtle...but never a Marlene...how the fuck do you explain a Marlene?

What the fuck am I thinking about? The old days, it was like just yesterday to me, a twenty-five-year-old Cancerian talking about the old days like I was born in Civil War times...twenty-five years old, too old to be young, too young to be old. But what the fuck does it matter!?...the wind sang in his skull...what the fuck! Everything is

163

yesterday, yesterdays, walking block after block, not up or down a street filled with people but through an alley, an alley filled, in summer, with watermelon rinds, corn cobs with no kernels left...cobs that he pushed nails into, at one end, chicken feathers into, at the other end, to make darts.

The alley, it clicked in his mind as he watched people's faces going the opposite way...the alley running parallel to Roosevelt Road...filled with, aside from rinds and cobs, everything an active, curious mind would need: condoms with semen tied up inside, fornicating mongrel cats, books printed in Hebrew, old-fashioned steam irons, rats with fangs as large as pencils, rats who had grown fat and old and feared nothing, bags of popsicle sticks, battered musical instruments, a ring carved out of wood, marbles, ball bearings, pants, shirts, hats, scarves, dishes, spoons, magazines from Germany, a rear view into the shops of people who pressed, sewed, sold, cooked, ate, defecated, lived!...ants who dragged crusts of bread away to heaven...or wherever it was that they dragged it, mysterious packages wrapped in Christmas paper, box loads of envelopes with the flaps missing, and once...like a rare treasure, he had picked up a diary, the life story of an Italian woman whose husband had been killed three weeks after they were married twenty years ago.

The alley in summer filled with rodents and treasures but did not seem so in the winter. The snow and ice in the winter time seemed to make the alley a kind of fairy land.

James pursed his lips together, trying not to look goofy, walking west on Forty-seventh Street, remembering how he had once run up the sides of garbage piled up in the alley, frozen, iced up garage...ran up and down quickly, pretending that he was on a mountain. And with him, through it all, was his dog Dukes...actually his aunt's dog...but to the world of the alley, it was James and Dukes.

Dukes, the proudest, blackest, baddest li'l dog anybody ever owned, was supposed to have been fed gunpowder in his youth and would attach a brick if he didn't like its shape. Li'l ol' bad ass Dukes, half fice, one part bull terrier and stuck together with little rippling grape bunches of muscle that seemed to glisten through his Chihuahua coat; Dukes, who would jump a cat of any size, snap his back in his jaws...be willing to take a few gashes on the nose as a testimonial to his feline killing commitment and still hang on 'til the cat—and there had been some fierce ones—was worried to death and left to rot, all fiercely ripped fur and blood.

Roaming up and down the alley gave James a certain rep in the family, one that bordered on the fringes of a rough joke that was bandied about whenever he wasn't.

"Y'all know where James is?" one of his cousins would ask, and the stock answer, with a nasty little grin, would be, "Walkin' up and down the alley with Dukes, that's where." "Either that or he's out in the coal cellar," the third party might push in, causing everybody to share maximum chuckles.

Out in the coal cellar, the dungeon beneath the sidewalk where coal was dumped through the manhole in the autumn, directly across from the front door to the four rooms and two closets where he and a number, too large a number for that space, had sweltered in summer, froze in the winter and almost suffocated in the spring, when the rank smell of ripe sewage would press in on them from all around.

Eleven fifty Washburne Avenue, in the coal celler, hesitantly reading the magazines, books and newspapers he'd gleaned up and down the alley, by the single shaft of light that streamed through the half dollar sized hole in the manhole cover, seated on a lumpy pile of hard coal.

The memory of the dark walls of the coal cellar, bleeding,

165

swiveling, rippling, crawling things and the foul odor of the place caused him to involuntarily screw up his face into a grimace...forcing two respectable looking middle-aged sisters passing him to edge over toward the sidewalk's edge.

Lawwwd, did you see that?'' one whispered loudly to the other, when they thought they were out of range.

"Uh huhhh, nice lookin' young fella too, on that wine, talkin' to theyselves...really hate to see that.''

Impulsively, James trotted back towards them, his creative juices bubbling, "I ain't on nothin', ladies," he spoke loudly and clearly. "I ain't *on* nothin'...nothin' but my people, my folks, if you wanna call that being *on* somethin'. I'm out here, in a groove, can you dig that?''

The two ladies, looking anxiously over their shoulders at him, scared shitless, picked up their lock step and hurried on, muffling startled, embarrassed smiles.

James shook his head sadly, mumbling..."People don't know the difference between somebody feeling good and somebody feeling bad...goddamn! People sure are fucked up.''

He reversed his direction, straightened himself up against a lamppost, stared up at the name of the street sign. St. Lawrence, surprised that he had walked so far.

Forty-seventh and St. Lawrence...a block down the street from Miss Sweet's house, across the hallway from Shirley, Ramona and Ellen...three of the most beautiful Black women he'd ever known, black and beautiful for this, that, or any other time...like...well, hell...one of them had cried for two hours watching John Payne and Maureen O'Hara pretend that they knew what reality was...that's how beautiful they were.

He crossed the street to the liquor store on the corner, feeling the urge to keep his high on.

And later, stopping in the Palm Tree Tavern, to

166

surreptitiously nurse his bottle in the toilet, his head flipped back to the basement as he flushed the toilet.

Eleven fifty Washburne, where, in the spring, when the winter snows melted, in addition to the sewer drainage smell, the murky waters would flush rats and their spring litters out, swirling them past, screeching, as members of the household would stand on milk crates and try to bash their heads in with heavy sticks. Year after year they swam past, some with crushed eyes, broken fangs and gnarled wounds from the year before.

James turned the bottle up for another long series of swallows before tossing it in the trash and weaving out into the bar. He slid onto a stool, ordered a glass of Bristol Cream and stared, fascinated in his wine haze, at the hundreds of bottles twinkling at him on the other side of the bar. His eyes, swimming up from the bottles, up to his reflection in the mirror, took him into the things happening behind and to each side of him...couples at tables, a pretty man in a blue velvet suit parading slowly by and two fast young sisters sitting to the left of him. He raised his glass in debonair fashion to their images in the mirror and sipped a silent toast, which they both saw but chose to ignore.

"Another Bristol, please."

He watched the wine being poured, liked the sight of the darkness of it filling up the clear glass, paid, and, with an even more elaborate, almost stately gesture, turned his eyes away from the mirror and held his glass up again...."Sisters...ladies?"

Both of them swiveled their heads his way, the one closest to him leaning back a bit, as though to capture and measure his full image.

"Sisters...I would like to offer y'all a quiet li'l toast in nutty wine...for being so close to me, for being who and what you are...."

167

They stared at him for another long moment, having taken the measure, caught the wine fumes, and then dissolved into indulgent smiles.

"Who do you think we are and what do you think we are?" the one closest to him, her long plastic eyelashes flicking at him cynically, asked.

James focused his eyes, looked them up and down, taking in their fox-furred wigs, the bangled necks, the jacked up boozums, the cold glints in their merciless eyes and retreated, unsure of what he should say, because he did know who and what they were, garbage cans for anybody's cum, seminal spittoons, 'hoes, but found himself incapable of saying the word.

His stomach suddenly began to churn as he drained his glass, nodded sickly to the two women and slid off the bar stool and stumbled out of the bar and into the deep twilight, swallowing and re-swallowing to try to hold down the puke.

Standing across the alley from the tavern he fought to gain control of himself by breathing deeply.

"Goddamn right you drunk, man," a hip, middle-aged dude said to him graciously, passing by, smiling at the sight of James leaning against the corner of an alley.

A couple young dudes, prowling, casually paused across the sidewalk from him, legs spaced in hip stances, watching and whispering intently to each other.

"Mannnnn...that motherfucker is sho' 'nuff trippin' out...ain't he?"

"Really!"

James, feeling danger vibrate across to him, pulled himself together with one long intake of air and walked away, still fighting nausea but determined to make it to the bus stop across the street and home, home, where he could take his shoes off and lay out, worn out from his walking, drinking and thinking.

Weeks Later. . .

Marlene lay in bed, hands laced behind her head, looking at the day. One advantage, she thought, about living on the sixth floor is that you can see a lot more.

She propped herself up and looked sharply at the highrise across from her, separated at the ground level by a parking lot and fifty yards of excessively well-manicured grass. The greenest ever seen.

As usual, the two men sat across from each other in the breakfast nook, sipping their first coffees and gesturing animatedly.

We have a breakfast nook too, just like theirs, and a living room and two bedrooms too, just like theirs. . .I'll bet they pay less rent though.

The idea was amusing to her, the idea that she, her mother and Mr. Ross would be paying more rent than the two white fags across the way. . .discrimination! That's what it would be. But, of course, it couldn't be...since everyone was treated equally in the complex, for better or worse.

Her gaze shifted to the fat Black woman in the apartment above the white faggots, the one who popped out of bed every morning doing strenuous exercises and, immediately afterwards, cooked a huge breakfast.

She unlaced her hands and stretched, yawning. Wonder who looks in on me?

The thought forced her arms down. She knew of the existence of several pairs of binoculars that always seemed to be trained in her direction.

Why wasn't James at home last night...?

Feeling reckless, she popped out of bed suddenly, shortie p.j. set clinging to her, put on her robe and padded from her room in bare feet to get a glass of orange juice.

The dream woke him up in a deep sweat...a huge, muscular figure with a baby's bald head and face was strangling him...mumbling all the while..."You killed me...you killed me...you killed me..." He sat up, dumped a cigarette from the pack near his bed into his hand, lit it, trembling.

Hmmf! Wonder what the fuck that was all about?..."You killed me...you killed me...you..."

The early promise of a hot day had been fulfilled...he stared blankly at the clock...12:00 and not a breeze stirring anywhere...a slow, dead, sultry, humid haze...July...in Chi.

He stared at the ringing phone for four hard rings...puzzled at why someone should be calling anyone else on a day as hot as this one was.

"Hello...James?"

"Hey, baby...what's happenin'?"...God. I almost asked who it was...

170

"Nothing much...I just felt like speaking to you...no, let me put it this way, to be honest...I felt like listenin' to your voice...I felt like hearing someone say something positive to me."

"Momma givin' you a bad time?"

After a long, dry pause...."Maybe not so much Momma as myself."

"What's that mean?" he asked, knowing already...the feeling playing around in his head too.

"Ohhh,...I don't know, lots of things...I guess."

"Run it down to me," he said, and eased down in the bed, beads of perspiration on his forehead.

"I called you last night," she replied, shifting the stream of conversation.

"I was out with a couple buddies of mine," he slid in easily..."we made one of those jam session things on the westside." Damn...you mean I have to lie about where I was?...guess so...how could I tell her I was fucking an old pregnant girlfriend on welfare in the projects?

"Oh," she said dryly.

A cool silence settled between them for a few seconds, an awkward silence.

"What were you goin' to say?" he blurted out.

"About what?"

"About something botherin' you,"...wiping the perspiration from his forehead, frowning hatefully at the lonely fly buzzing around. Yeahhh, go 'head and put it into any kind of form you want to put it into. I woke up with doubts in my head today too...to put it mildly.

"There's nothing bothering me...really,"...a dead, clammy pause, and then, "We really are takin' a big step, aren't we?"

The perspiration beading up again...a small trickle running down his back...damn it's hot!

171

"It's the biggest one I've taken so far, in my life."

"Me too!" she answered, with nervous quickness.

"Are you...are you having second thoughts...doubts about...?"

"No, are you?"

Yes, yes, yes, yes, yes...goddamnit! Yes! Every kind of doubt in the world.

"No," he answered firmly.

Marlene took a deep breath, feeling relieved, her confidence jacked up. Momma be damned!

"It makes me happy to hear you say that."

"Would it make you even happier if I said that I love you and that I'm lookin' forward to being with you, to sharing my life with you, to groovin' with you?"

"A li'l bit," she said, her confidence jacked even higher, and laughed, her spirits perking.

"Well, I'm saying it...and a whole bunch of other thangs...but they'll have to wait for another time."

"I can wait..."

The silence settled back in, warmer, briefer this time.

"Marlene...?"

"Yessss?"

"Ain't it hot out today!?"

"I don't know. I haven't been out yet, but I guess I'll find out soon enough."

"You goin' to work early?"

"Nope...goin' downtown, to do some shoppin'."

And the bride was dazzling in her lacy white veil...

"What for...anything special?"

"Not really. I don't suppose it matters to you...but, are you aware that you only have one skillet?"

"Hmf!...never even thought about it."

"Well, I did...and you also need some plates and some knives 'n forks...and..."

172

"Well git on yo' job, woman!"

"I am...I am...I am...as soon as I..."

"Don't let me hang you up...git on!"

"Ooo, James?"

"Yeah baby?"

"Momma wants to fix lunch for you...for us tomorrow...her last line of defense."

"Dig it...before or after you move."

"Before..."

"I was goin' to ask you, what time do you want me to come over?"

"How about 11:30?"

"Sounds good. What're we havin' for lunch?"

"I don't know, who cares?"

"I don't."

"Me neither...

"I'll see you tomorrow then."

"Right...tomorrow...11:30."

"James?"

The busy fly settled on the sheet beside him, he swatted at it with his free hand, unsuccessfully.

"Yes ma'am," he answered, facetiously.

"I'm going to try to be the best woman I know how to be to you."

"I know you are, baby," the seriousness of what she had said choking him up. "I know you are," he replied, trying to push a lightness into the words that he didn't feel.

"See you tomorrow."

"Take care, baby...and don't buy too many forks, remember...there ain't but two of us."

"Don't worry...I'll just buy enough for us and whoever might be comin' to dinner sometime."

"'Bye now..."

"'Bye."

173

He hung up the telephone, drenched with perspiration, doubt and indecision. Damn it's hot!

Mrs. Ross (ex-Cole) stared at her daughter's back sadly...if only her father had lived long enough...here she is, gettin' ready to go off and live with some jobless artist, forgetting everything that we ever did for her, the piano lessons, the sacrifices that were made to make sure that she didn't have to suffer, would never have the problem of dealing with the hardships Isaac and I...God Rest His Soul...had to deal with.

"Marlene...honey...sit 'n talk for a minute!"

"I'm in a hurry, Momma...I have some shoppin' to do before I go to work."

"I know you can spare five minutes."

"What is it, Momma?" Marlene asked, a hard, cold tone in her voice.

Lord in heaven...what's this younger generation coming to? Whatever happened to that decent, upstanding young man, what was his name, Paul...Paul Hollis...young Negro on his way up...now he...I would've been proud to have him as a son-in-law. And what is she going to give me? Some rascal I've never seen, some scamp she's going off to live common law with...I'll have bastards for grandchildren.

"What is it, Momma...? I told you I've got some shoppin' to do," Marlene asked, urgently.

Mrs. Ross slumped into one of her highrise, Bauhaus-styled, living room chairs and began to cry...

"Don't cry, Momma," Marlene said to her, touched to the quick, "please don't cry."

The unbelievably sweet, tender voice of Roberta Flack singing "Angelitos Negroes" cooed out at James as he

174

scribbled..."The Textures of Niggers...

"A voice, an atmosphere, us...msuri sane, Afro-honey...Swahili, Twi, Ga, Ghana, Gold Coast, Slavery, us...uh huh. A woman, mine...Black, us...babies maybe...Black too, no rhetoric, just conception, nipples and milk...Black too, maybe...if possible.

"A music in the rhythm of the conception, the black ghost of a child within all us Black Americans...the art of our lives. A good feelin'...a groove for real livin'...condemned by unreal people, unfortunately white people...for them that is...in the final analysis...but that ain't nothing to be really concerned about, it's us first, to be considered...fuck them! Our texture...in all the textures we come in...from light cream to deep coffee...night and day.

"Living and loving for a day and a way that has nothing to do with taller buildings and more, and bigger phallic symbols... Living and loving for living and loving...for Bird Being Bird and Miles Being Miles and all the rest of our Black heroes, both living and thought to be dead...programmed into a grave that they never could be found in.

"A soft, sweet, velvet touch...the moisture of thick lips on effervescent souls, undiminished by all of the fears punched against us."

James took a long pull on the bottle of stout, the heavy, cold, malt flavor of it coursing into him like a dark stream of benzedrine tablets...damn, it's hot!

"Life, love, rhythm, women and facts...a dangerous juxtaposition of compatibles...a coexistence of ideas that never seem to fix peace in place...not in America, not where Bird blew 'Laura' and Wallace sang 'Segregation Forever'...the texture of niggers...a romance born of necessity, nailed into place by lullabies from a Black

175

woman's tongue, polished by Black asses rubbing up against cold white lips, senseless tongues, unable to deal with anything spicier than salt, no p-p-pepper please!

"The texture of niggers...no huge bronze earrings, ten-hour corn rows and bubas from Hong Kong...no real need for false grace and excessive charm...just grits and the nitty gritty...meaning, for the illiterate, a honey dark titty...a moisturized, smoothly sculptured sister with teakwood nipples in her soul and a long, dark scream...

"Marlene..."

He shook the foam out of the bottle into his mouth, sweat gluing his undershirt to his body, and went to the refrigerator for a fresh, cold bottle...

"The texture of niggers...the texture of niggers...more than song, dance and soul...

"Rich shit, too brown and good for an earth plagued by commercials sponsoring fake shit...

"The texture of niggers...dancing inside a bleeding heart, conquering madness with a sway of the hips, cancelling subscriptions to genocidal notions with the act of loving...even after the baby had been made...

"The dazzling counterpoint of extended measures...not just for your time, but an expanded beat, the bridging of a dreadful, deep, shark-fed ocean...fed for centuries with African bodies and white hatred...a New World counterpoint, Afro-American pleasure...an Afro-American woman, a New World treasure...

"Not the designer of the cloth but an unmistakable part of the fabric...a vital part of the texture...the texture of niggers."

He stopped, to drink more beer, having run out of steam...and ran back through the words, silently reviewing all of Marlene's bad points as he did so.

Awww, what's the use! I love the bitch! Even if she ain't

perfect, who is?

The idea that he would have to be, in a sense, approved of by her mother rankled him.

A twenty-five-year-old woman paying that much attention to what her mother said. Shit! I'm twenty-five too and I haven't paid that much attention to what anybody in my family thought or said...for years.

The afternoon melted into evening...a slow, dead, warm, wet transference...leaving the un-air conditioned sections of the city ripe for an expression of repressed grievances, riots, in other words.

James, with good timing, got to the florist shop five minutes before closing.

"Where do you want these delivered, young man?" the florist asked, a wreath of wrinkles circling his coffee-brown face.

James gave him Pearline's address again, slowly, patiently.

"We don't get very many orders for roses in that area," the man said, and ha ha-ed in a supercilious manner.

James' sullen expression cancelled any other would-be jokes.

"How long will it take to get them over?"

"Not too long, I'll have my boy deliver them on his way home, he lives in that area...uhhh...is there a card with these?"

"Yeah...why not?" he answered, and scribbled quickly..."I wish...I wish...love, always, James."

The florist glanced at the card, annoyed to not be able to figure out the message, accepted payment for two dozen American Beauty roses and prepared to close his shop.

James wandered back through the shopping plaza on his way back home, stood staring through the plate glass window of the coffee shop at Reena performing her duties and decided not to tempt fate by having a hamburger...continued strolling through the humid evening air, feeling very special about himself because he was a writer.

His feelings took him toward the lakefront, moving upstream through the waves of commuters piling out of the I.C. station, refugees from hard-fought wars in the Loop.

He paused for a drink in one of those tricky little bars just past the point of confusion about whether or not they wanted to serve what they thought of as "Negroes." They knew they did not...but the law and geography worked against them.

"What'll it be?" the bartender asked him sourly.

"Double gin and a li'l tonic."

"I know my business," the bartender told him and stalked away to slosh the mixture together...

Racist motherfucker...

He sat, looking around...checked out the obligatory, middle-aged white woman with the I-been-a-lush-for-twenty-years look, the brooding Irishman, the trying-in-the-late-afternoon couple, trying, lamely, to ignore his presence, and a few lousy stragglers scattered up and down the bog.

The bartender splashed the top inch from the drink as he slammed it down in front of him...

James' first impulse was to slop the drink into the bartender's face but he decided not to, better be cool, he reasoned, it would really be a trip to be in jail on the night before my wedding...the night before my...o wowww...!

He paid for the drink and left it sitting there, afraid that the bartender may have spat in it or something.

Hands clasped behind him, he strolled along the lake's perimeter...the balmy breezes sailing from across the water into his face...reviewing his past and his future in the slightly ruffling waves. Chinua Achebe...yes, Achebe said it, things do fall apart...the Aquarian Age, a Cancerian in

178

the Aquarian Age...born into a Black family that never had any concern for or any doubts about its blackness...too bad so many young sisters and brothers are growing up these days with such a hell of an identity crisis going on, despite the fact that they are relating more and more to...Blackness?-niss?-nuss?-nizz?

Writing...becoming aware, perceptive, imaginative, artless, skillful...jobless...

Got to get in touch with Willie tomorrow about that gig he was talking about...

They were within twenty yards of him before his eyes turned away from the blinking, illusionary lights dangling on the water, far out in the lake...two sisters, both short, brown skinned and feisty, exquisitely corn rowed, the patterns even more striking because of the dull reflections from the lake on the bare skull areas between the braiding.

The words sang themselves out of him before he had a chance to effectively measure sounds and effects. "And how are you two beautiful sisters this lovely evenin'?"

The sister closest to him eased over a wee much as they passed, niggers in the failing light, American-bred paranoia... He turned to look at their outlines, at the lush bottoms and carefully tended waistlines...and they looked back over their shoulders at him, measuring emotions and distances.

He shook his head sadly from side to side...yeahhh...I can dig it...gotta stay on your job at all times...

Things do fall apart, down and lots of times...out.

He settled himself onto one of the huge, lakeside blocks and stared at the point between sky, horizon and lake.

Writing...me...writing...what could be a stranger occupation? "I saw 'im...yes indeed...I saw 'im...clear as day, sittin' out on the back porch...jest scribblin' his buns off."

"Maybe he had some homework?"

"Now you know good 'n well that they don't give them kids no homework in the fifth grade...not at that school noway."

"James! James Wright...have you been listening closely to our story?"

"Yes, Mizz Brophy."

"Well, then...if you have, give the class a brief synopsis of what the story was about."

"A brief what?"

"Snicker...snicker snicker...tee hee hee."

"Aww haw haw haw...ha ha ha."

"Quiet class!...tell us, in your own words, what you thought the story was about."

"Well...this li'l boy..."

"What was his name, James?"

"Uhhh..."

"Well, what was it?"

"Li'l Black Sambo...,"

"Tee hee, haw haw...ha ha ha...snicker."

..."You little black son of a bitch."

..."Nigger!"

..."Nigger!"

..."Niggers ain't shit!"

..."Nigger!"

..."Niggger!"

..."Black...nigggg...er!"

..."James Wright Junior!...don'tchu never let me hear you call nobody black again, you heah me?"

..."Black is Beautiful."

..."Niggggger...!"

He eased away from the stone, brushing dust from his pants, thinking about Pearline and the recent evening on her front step and then, within.

180

Pearline...Marlene...

God, why couldn't Marlene have some Pearline in her and why couldn't Pearline have some Marlene in *her*...but I guess if that were the case, Pearline wouldn't be Pearline and Marlene wouldn't be Marlene. Awww shiiii-it!

He found himself scaling the rocks of the Point...going up the peninsular section of the rocks to the top, remembering, unafraid, wishing for somebody to bust in the mouth or stomp...for the unwanted disturbance of that evening.

He reached the top section of the rocks, the path back to the city in front of him, the lake, ruffling slightly more now, with deep evening coming in, behind him.

He took the path to the city, nodding folksily to Mediterranean brothers in ermine, sharkskin and leopard wool, blew his hot breath at ebullient sisters with fresh black beer foam coating their skulls and curled the tip ends of his lips down like he was the Tumb Tumb of Dwewyiee Bop, Afro-American branch.

Now...what had happened? he asked himself, trying to shake the fuzziness out of his brain and answer the phone at the same time...I was walking to the tunnel, on my way home...minding my own business...o yeahhh...and then I ran into...

"Hello."

"Hello, James?!"

"Marlene!?"

"Yes, who did you think it was!? Are you comin' or not?"

"Whoa! Whoa! Hold on, baby...take it slow...am I...?" O...o...o...Gawwwd!

"It's 1:30."

"It is!....look...I'll...why don't you come pick...?"

"Why don't I do what?"

181

"Uhhh, never mind! I'll see you in fifteen minutes."

"I thought you said you were gonna be here for lunch?"

"I'll be there baby, I'll be there!"

James slammed the phone down quickly...holding his head with his free hand...

What....had...happened?

He jammed himself off of the bed and hastily, clumsily, began to try to pull himself together...

Having hastily pulled a pair of pants on, slipped an undershirt down over his chest and, while standing in front of the mirror, trying to shave, he started laughing...

"Heyyy brotherrrrr...what's happenin'...?" the slender, young brother had said to him, looking vaguely familiar.

"You got it, blood," James had replied, "you got it," and then they had both stared at each other, trying to recall the circumstances because they remembered each other.

After a quick bunch of doubtful people and places had been memory-milked, on both sides, they leaned into each other, thumbs up, for the shake of cohesion that confirmed that they...they had been there...*that night.* The night of the pigs. "La Noche de los Puercos," the young brother had called it, surprisingly. And invited him to a set.

The set...young, Black, gifted...poets and musicians in a basement.

"How often do you brothers get together?"

"Hard to say...but we do sho' 'nuff try to be off into it on Tuesday."

"Uhh, why Tuesday?"

"Tuesday? Why Tuesday?...I don't know. I guess somebody thought Tuesday was a hip day to session on...you know? I mean, like...everybody does a thing on Saturday, or Friday, or Sunday...anyhow...but nobody gets a thing together on Tuesday...so, that's what we be doin'...Tuesday."

182

Tuesday night...from 8:38 to 5:44...

"So...you're going to steal our daughter away from us, huh?" met him, as he turned the cold, precisely measured geometric corner of the apartment...

On his job now, cheap wine headache receding..."No, not really, Mrs. Ross,...I'm just offerin' you a chance not to have a son-in-law...in law, if you can dig where I'm comin' from."

Marlene coughed nervously behind her hand, knowing how humorless her mother could be, and then broke in lightly..."It's awfully hot, James, can I fix you a drink?"

"Why not," he said, settling into a severely tailored chair, into his groove..."yeah, why not?"

Marlene, knowing her man, and accurately judging his cockiness, eased away from Mother and Man to mix strong gin 'n tonics.

"Marlene tells us you write, have you sold anything?"

Listen to this ol' jiveass broad talk this white movie star bullshit to me!

James turned his most dazzling, artificial smile on her and announced, "No, no...I have not decided to release any of my work yet."

Mrs. Ross looked at him respectfully, wrinkling the corner of her left eye a bit...

Marlene quickly moved back onto the set with a trio of glasses...on a cocktail serving tray...

Mmmmm...ain't we swank?

"Uhh, do you think there is a possibility of earning a good living from writing...these days?" Mrs. Ross asked, sipping her drink. James, sipping coolly on the hair of the dog that had bitten him last night..."I don't see why not."

James stared at Mrs. Ross, above the transparent edge of his drink, knowing, as her eyes met his, that he had beaten

183

the house, knowing that he had gotten slightly past the "Negro" facade. He looked casually at Marlene, wishing that they were alone...

"Marlene tells me that you just got back from Vietnam?"

"Yes'um," he replied, putting her on lightly, irritating her by implying age in his answer, egged on a bit by the gin dropping to the pit of his gut, mingling with the residue from last night... "I was there...lived, loved and died a li'l bit over there. But everybody who's ever been there, fightin' the white man's racist war, did the same thing. It's a helluva place to be."

He crossed his legs, straightened his back and took another long sip. Mrs. Ross followed suit, liking and disliking the arrogance she saw in him.

They sat calmly eyeing each other, circling.

"You and Marlene are taking a big step," she said, in a matter of fact voice.

"We know," he replied, looking at how beautiful Marlene was with the sunshine glinting off the planes of her face.

"Naturally, I can't tell you all what to do since you're both grown...but I can say this...I don't think too much of the way you're going about it...I..."

"Momma...!"

"No, no!...go on, Mrs. Ross, speak your piece," he shushed Marlene's interjection and waved Mrs. Ross on.

"Like I've said, both of you all are grown, so it serves no purpose to try to tell you what to do...all I can say is this, I don't think either one of you has given enough consideration to a whole bunch of things."

"Like what, Mrs. Ross?" James asked, quietly.

"Well, for one thing...children."

"We don't plan to have any," Marlene said.

"At least, not for awhile anyway," James added.

Mrs. Ross nursed her drink, frowning slightly as she

swallowed. "Whenever...but eventually you'll have bastards, is that fair to me?" she directed her question to Marlene.

Uhn huh...we be gettin' down to the nitty gritty now, huh?

"Momma, if, and when, we do have kids, to us they'll be our babies, anybody else can call them whatever they want to." James saw with a glance that Marlene's glass was three fourths empty.

"I know both of you all are sitting there thinking of me in the worst way possible...but I don't care, we raised Marlene to be somebody and..."

"You don't think she can be somebody with me?"

"You don't even have a job," Mrs. Ross shot at him viciously, "and from all I've heard, you don't seem to be interested in getting one."

"Not if it means working my life away, instead of doing my life's work."

"Does that suppose to mean that your wife works her life away?" Mrs. Ross came back at him, with heat.

Marlene quietly collected their glasses for fresh drinks, feeling absolute confidence in her man's ability to handle it...to take care of business.

"No, that's not what it's supposed to mean, Mrs. Ross...and that's not what I'm implying. So far as jobs go, I have an offer for a job with the County...I am thinking through all the possibilities before I get into it 'cause I don't want anything or anybody to interfere with my writing."

'Round the corner, in the kitchen alcove, Marlene smiled at the bristling tone of James' voice.

"You're really serious about writing, aren't you?" Mrs. Ross asked, cooling herself out.

"As serious as I am about Marlene, maybe more."

The three of them sat uncomfortably for a few long

185

moments, trying to pretend that the scene didn't exist, Marlene and James trying to figure out the proper form for gettin' on, under the circumstances.

Mrs. Ross looked over her shoulder at the streets...sadly, "I don't know, maybe I'm just old fashioned, I guess...but living together instead of being married always just seemed so common to me."

Marlene went over and kissed her mother warmly on the cheek...

"Momma, didn't you once tell me that the most important thing was to be happy with the man you love, didn't you?"

"Yes, yes I did...but I didn't think that you would take that to mean that...that you should go off and live with him."

"I'm happy with this man, Momma...and we want to be together and," glancing at James, "we don't want to be married...we're not tryin' to do anything to spite anybody, we just want to do things our way."

Mrs. Ross looked keenly, directly into her daughter's eyes and began to cry, softly and quietly at first, but then, completely...tears gushing out.

"Marlene...Marlene...my baby...myyy baybee...I've been lookin' forward so long, so long to a big church weddin'...with bridesmaids and organ music, and a big reception and..."

James eased over to the other side of Mrs. Ross, stared across her head lowered to Marlene's chest, into Marlene's eyes...

"Mrs. Ross...I love Marlene and I intend to do everything I can to make her life with me a happy one. It's obvious that you don't think too much of me, and I think that's because you don't know me. If I were you, I would put a lot more confidence into my daughter's choice...I know, from loving her and being with her, that she's nobody's fool. In my

186

family, they've always given the women credit for creatin' mother wit...I think you're short-changin' your own teachings by assuming that I might not be the right man for your daughter.''

James stopped, suddenly very high. Marlene pursed her lips into an imaginary kiss and Mrs. Ross straightened up, drying her eyes. She turned to James with a little smile on her face... ''You even talk like a writer, don't you?''

''Sometimes, when it's necessary,'' he smiled back, breathing in her perfume up close.

Melvin Ross let himself in, home from the office early, paused in the door at the sound of male laughter blending with that of his wife and stepdaughter...who?

He rubbed his mustache down, cleared his throat and prepared himself mentally to meet this young whippersnapper Marlene was running away with.

The warmth of the tableau shook him...Marlene, bubbling, his wife and the young whippersnapper all sitting on the sofa by the window, his window, drinking his good gin and obviously having a good time. ''Com' on in, Melvin...com' on in!...don't stand over there starin' with your eyes popped out!...I want you to meet Marlene's young man. James, this is my husband Melvin.''

James stood coolly, to receive him...sooooo, this is the lecherous ol' bastard himself.

''How do you do, Mr. Ross?''

''Uhh, fine...just fine...''

''The novel concerns two older people...ages roughly forty-eight and fifty-two. I give several reasons for the age thing being what it is: (1) an assumption is often made in the Youth Era (now) that older folks do not fall in love, make love, or have love affairs, (2) another assumption is that, for all the reasons that have been propagandized...any

187

discussion of a generation gap implies that it is the old who do not understand the young...almost never is this reversed, (3) the two lovers in the piece are Black, which is purely another dimension altogether...if for no other reason than that the Black stud-dude is always thought of as twenty and no older than thirty, ever. Same goes for the super-oversexed chick.''

Marlene tipped up to peek over James' left shoulder, the bag of groceries in her arms giving her away with its rustling.

"Hey baby," he turned to receive her kiss, "I didn't hear you come in."

"From the look of the wrinkles of concentration on the back of your head, you probably couldn't hear, period...how's it goin'?''

James, grateful for a break, turned from his drawing board desk, "I'm deep off into it."

Marlene smiled indulgently and began to move energetically about the kitchen, putting groceries away, plotting a dinner, talking across the distance from James' writing nook to the kitchen.

"You think they'll dig it...the love story?''

"Why not? *Another Place* is sellin' pretty good...and ain't that the name of the game?...and besides, if they don't dig it, what the fuck do I care?''

Marlene paused in the doorway between the kitchen and living room, munching on a carrot..."A...munch munch crunch...Black love story is really kind of off beat. What makes it a...munch....Black...munch...love story anyway?''

James rolled his eyes back up into his head...just like her to put that kind of weight on my ass...just like her... "They do, baby...they do!'' he said, shutting off the conversation, and turned back to map out his guidelines for... *The Sweeter The Juice.*

188

"Ohh Jammes!" Marlene called to him excitedly, breaking his concentration again..."Guess what?!"

"What?" he asked, loving her, teasing her.

"I passed that exam...the one in urban statistics...the one I told you I knew I would fail in."

He turned around to watch her bustling from refrigerator to sink..."Shit! You oughta have passed it, I told you that...all you had to do was estimate how many niggers they got jammed up in these inner city traps!"

Marlene shook a stalk of celery at him, laughing..."James!...you!...you!..." and lacking the words to deal with him, returned to her salad fixing.

He turned back to his notes, smiling, wondering if he'd have to do six drafts of the piece he was starting on, like *Another Place*, puzzling over where the different sections would come in, and how he would deal with them, feeling tired of the work to come, already.

"How do you want your steak?" she called to him, "this is my last disturbance! I promise!"

Damn, you'd think a woman would know how a man wanted his steak, after almost two years together.

"Medium well, baby...medium well...with lots o' love."

Two years almost...hmmmmm...they say the first two are the hardest, after that it's supposed to be jelly...if only we could keep her mother from visiting so goddamned often...*The Sweeter The Juice*. He turned slowly, meditatively...to stare at Marlene's back, one hand on a well-turned hip, a fork turning meat in the other hand, looking good, taking care of business.

Looks like me 'n the sister might have a nice thang goin' on up in here...

189

CONSPIRACY

BY ODIE HAWKINS

Henrik Malan was the cold and ruthless South African government secret agent who devised the plan to have the Black American ghettos destroy themselves from within by supplying them with a cheap but highly addictive drug known on the street as "ghetto blaster." And what would South Africa gain? The discredit of Nelson Mandella, a public relations coup and credibility in the eyes of the world. Usually Odie Hawkins, to the delight of his thousands of fans, uses his life experience for the basis of his books. Here he relies on his considerable ability as a storyteller to relate a deadly tale of intrigue and high adventure.

BLACK BAIT

BY LEO GUILD

She's passionate, bold, and goes after what she wants. And what she wants is you! Or, to put that another way, your money. Sure, she's got a dazzling smile; and she's a master of kinky sex. But underneath that kittenish exterior is a petulant and mercurial woman—a woman who alw s gets what she wants. One way or the other...Leo Guild, author of the best-selling *The Girl Who Loved Black*, tells the true and shocking story of a gambling woman with a heart of gold, nerves of steel and backbone of ice. You'll never forget Lila!

AIN'T GOT TIME TO DIE

BY NOLAN DAVIS

Set against the background of black middle-class dreams, lust, greed and affluence, the book depicts the rise of LAWRENCE XAVIER JORDAN from the depths of the ghetto to wealth, power and respect. Along the way, Jordan encounters a gallery of characters as unique and entertaining as any ever drawn by Ralph Ellison or James Baldwin. There is SOUTHWALL LOVINGOOD, a pulsating, 300 pounds of appetite for whiskey, ham-hocks and greens and beautiful, hot-blooded women. CLARE, Jordan's mother, is a fine example of a deserted woman who seeks life in the son who is a re-creation of her love for her husband. Voluptuous MARCELLA RONSOM is a turn-on to look at, but beneath her tropical surface, she's as cold as a slab in the morgue. *AIN'T GOT TIME TO DIE* is a rich, bright celebration of life!